PETER SOMMER TRAVELS

EXPERT-LED ARCHAEOLOGICAL & CULTURAL TOURS FOR SMALL GROUPS

TOUR OPERATOR OF THE YEAR

2015 Gold Award, 2016 Silver Award, 2017 Gold Award & 2018 Silver Award
- AITO (The Association of Independent Tour Operators)

ONE OF THE WORLD'S "TOP TEN LEARNING RETREATS"
- NATIONAL GEOGRAPHIC

EXPLORING IRELAND

EASTER IN ATHENS

EXPLORING SICILY

EXPLORING CRETE: ARCHAEOLOGY, NATURE AND FOOD

CRUISING THE LYCIAN SHORE

WALKING AND CRUISING SOUTHERN DALMATIA

ESCORTED ARCHAEOLOGICAL TOURS, GULET CRUISES AND PRIVATE CHARTERS

OMMER.COM

GRANTA

12 Addison Avenue, London W11 4QR | email: editorial@granta.com
To subscribe go to granta.com, or call 020 8955 7011 in the United Kingdom, 845-267-3031
(toll-free 866-438-6150) in the United States

ISSUE 151: SPRING 2020

GUEST EDITOR	Rana Dasgupta
DEPUTY EDITOR	Rosalind Porter
POETRY EDITOR	Rachael Allen
DIGITAL DIRECTOR	Luke Neima
MANAGING EDITOR	Eleanor Chandler
SENIOR DESIGNER	Daniela Silva
ASSISTANT EDITOR	Josie Mitchell
EDITORIAL ASSISTANT	Lucy Diver
COMMERCIAL DIRECTOR	Noel Murphy
OPERATIONS AND SUBSCRIPTIONS	Mercedes Forest
MARKETING	Aubrie Artiano, Simon Heafield
PUBLICITY	Pru Rowlandson, publicity@granta.com
CONTRACTS	Isabella Depiazzi
TO ADVERTISE CONTACT	Renata Molina Lopes Renata.Molina-Lopes@granta.com
FINANCE	Mercedes Forest, Sophia Themistocli, Elizabeth Wedmore
SALES MANAGER	Katie Hayward
IT MANAGER	Mark Williams
PRODUCTION ASSOCIATE	Sarah Wasley
PROOFS	Katherine Fry, Jessica Kelly, Lesley Levene, Jess Porter, Vimbai Shire, Martha Sprackland
CONTRIBUTING EDITORS	Anne Carson, Mohsin Hamid, Isabel Hilton, Michael Hofmann, A.M. Homes, Janet Malcolm, Adam Nicolson, Leanne Shapton, Edmund White
PUBLISHER AND EDITOR	Sigrid Rausing

This selection copyright © 2020 Granta Publications.

Granta, ISSN 173231 (USPS 508), is published four times a year by Granta Publications, 12 Addison Avenue, London W11 4QR, United Kingdom.

The US annual subscription price is $48. Airfreight and mailing in the USA by agent named WN Shipping USA, 156–15 146th Avenue, 2nd Floor, Jamaica, NY 11434, USA. Periodicals postage paid at Brooklyn, NY 11256.

US Postmaster: Send address changes to *Granta*, WN Shipping USA, 156–15 146th Avenue, 2nd Floor, Jamaica, NY 11434, USA.

Subscription records are maintained at *Granta*, c/o Abacus e-Media, 21 Southampton Row, London, WC1B 5HA.

Air Business Ltd is acting as our mailing agent.

Granta is printed and bound in Italy by Legoprint. This magazine is printed on paper that fulfils the criteria for 'Paper for permanent document' according to ISO 9706 and the American Library Standard ANSI/NIZO Z39.48-1992 and has been certified by the Forest Stewardship Council (FSC). *Granta* is indexed in the American Humanities Index.

ISBN 978-1-909-889-32-3

NEW FROM CAMBRIDGE UNIVERSITY PRESS

The Beats
A Literary History

Steven Belletto, *Lafayette College, Pennsylvania*

Kerouac. Ginsberg. Burroughs. These are the most famous names of the Beat Generation, but in fact they were only the front line of a much more wide-ranging literary and cultural movement. This critical history takes readers through key works by these authors, but also radiates out to discuss dozens more writers and their works, showing how they all contributed to one of the most far-reaching literary movements of the post-World War II era.

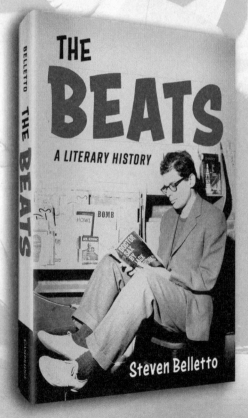

The
free entry and half-price tickets thank you very much indeed
Pass

National
Art Pass___

Elisabeth Bolzon
Individual

SEE MORE. FOR LESS.

Free entry to 240+ museums and galleries
50% off entry to major exhibitions
All for just £73 a year

Search National Art Pass

Art Fund_

Viktor Wynd, master of the contemporary Wunderkabin
with a collection of artefacts and curiosities that are mo
and wonderful than ever.

£35
Hardcover
200 pages with 160 colour illustrations
ISBN: 978-3791385198

Available now in all good bookshops

Edinburgh International Book Festival

15–31 August 2020

The World, in Words.
900 events featuring 1000 authors, poets, musicians and artists, plus cafés, bookshops and bars all in one central leafy tented village in Edinburgh's beautiful New Town.

Programme launch: 11 June
Tickets on sale: 27 June

edbookfest.co.uk
@edbookfest

FOSTER & SON

Foster & Son, making the finest bespoke boots and shoes in
St. James's, London since 1840. Our team of craftsmen maintain a
continuous tradition, using techniques unchanged for two centuries.

———

JERMYN STREET, ST JAMES'S, LONDON
FOSTER.CO.UK

CONTENTS

10 **Introduction**
Rana Dasgupta

TISSUE

15 **Newts**
Anita Roy

19 **Hold Your Fire**
Chloe Wilson

46 **Laxmi**
Anita Khemka

SELF

59 **The Station**
J. Robert Lennon

78 **Secondhand**
Mónica de la Torre

89 **Hair**
Mahreen Sohail

99 **Learning to Sing**
Lydia Davis

COLLECTIVE

109 **Snap**
Anouchka Grose

123 *from* **the knotweed sonnets**
Andrew McMillan

129 **You Are Here,
You Are Not a Ghost**
Mark Doty

NATION

147 **Diminishing Returns**
Fatin Abbas

157 **Crimes of Space**
*Eyal Weizman in conversation
with Rana Dasgupta*

175 **Border Documents**
Arturo Soto

195 **As if in Prayer**
Steven Heighton

SPECIES

205 **The Lake**
Kapka Kassabova

221 **Between Light and Storm**
Esther Woolfson

230 **Click-Wrap**
Ida Börjel

243 **All Species Have the
Same Life**
Emanuele Coccia

COSMOS

251 **Clarity**
Ruchir Joshi

270 **Already Two**
Vladimir Mayakovsky

271 **Notes on contributors**

The poems that introduce each section are by Tishani Doshi

Introduction

Increasingly, the word turns basic, its capillary complexity beaten out. A *membrane* gets you a dead, hermetic sheath: synthetic sheeting to insulate a building from moisture or fire; a plastic barrier against infection.

This may in fact be the most venerable meaning. Across history, the most impressive quality of skin and tissue – *membrana* – was impermeability. Leather, which could be used for carrying liquid or keeping out the rain, was a *membranum*. So was the scraped hide of parchment; as Isidore of Seville explained in the seventh century, 'because the kings of Pergamum lacked papyrus sheets, they first had the idea of using skins . . . These are also called *membrana* because they are stripped from the *members* of livestock.'

Membrana enclosed the body; they also blocked its apertures, repelling foreign insinuations. Sound bounced off the ear's *membranum tympani*. In Tudor England – as the playwright Ben Jonson described – Catholic continentals conspired in vain against the Protestant membrane that guarded the Virgin Queen cult: Elizabeth I 'had a membrana on her, which made her incapable of man, though for her delight she tryed many . . . ther was a French chirurgion who took in hand to cut it, yett fear stayed her, and his death.'

In later times, however, membranes became porous, and it was science that made them so. In 1826, Henri Dutrochet wrote excitedly about a new discovery, *osmosis*, which he had demonstrated by making differently concentrated fluids pass through a chicken intestine. 'At the outset,' he recalled, 'the specific objective of this work was to study the movement of sap in plants . . . This discovery led me much further than I had ever imagined. Indeed, in finding the mechanism and the cause of the movement of sap, I discovered the secret mechanism of vital movement [which belongs] equally to animals and plants.' So clear was it to Dutrochet that osmosis provided a physical explanation for life's mystery that he had to insist it was merely the *immediate* cause, and his faith in the *ultimate* cause – God – remained intact. But subsequent discoveries only vindicated his scientific awe. Under the microscope, the surface of tissues and fibres presented a marvellous array of ports and tunnels through which essential substances were exchanged. The twentieth century then unlocked the workings of life's fundamental unit – the cell – which was wrapped in an intricate double-layered membrane studded with protein hatches for moving molecules in and out. These movements created electrical and chemical gradients between cells – and *life energy*, it seemed, was nothing more than the resulting force field of currents and flows. Dutrochet was right: the secret of life was to be found in membranes, whose miraculous architecture allowed them to selectively absorb and repel.

Absorption and repulsion. No principles can be more fundamental than these. They arouse our greatest passions – and our greatest poems; societies brawl over their priority. We cherish communion, exchange and intercourse, of course, but also distance, seclusion and defence. Talk of membranes, therefore, is never entirely literal. If one era sees skin as an impenetrable shield, while another admires its permeability, the reason may lie in allegory.

In *Spheres*, his vast meditation on contemporary life, philosopher Peter Sloterdijk supposes that the European psyche took its modern form when the protective membrane of the celestial sphere disappeared. The Ptolemaic bubble burst, and the planet drifted, shell-less, in empty space. But human beings need to be insulated from the terror of meaninglessness; and if the modern era has resounded so with the din of *construction*, it is because all its overwrought energies have poured into replacing the shattered cosmic housing. We fend off exposure, most conspicuously, by mastering and domesticating the one sphere remaining to us, until the earth itself is turned into a giant security system of information, machines, markets and nations. But no matter how physical and solid these structures appear, their function is *symbolic* – and symbols may wear out, even while the material world remains pretty much unchanged. At moments of transition or crisis, our fabricated metaphysical shelters can shatter, and we are naked again.

Perhaps we are at such a moment today. The concentric spheres insulating much of the modern world appear to be ruptured, suddenly; alien forces seem to be flooding in. We are preoccupied by national borders, whose skin seems flimsy in the face of contemporary flows of money and people. The perimeters of the self are breached by computer incursions: privacy disappears, so does the uncluttered mind, and even the boundary between human and machine. The division between human and nature, meanwhile, is tragically trampled: the latter is overwhelmed, and the modern world's most cherished layer of security and consolation is lost. The planetary sphere itself turns against us: layers of the atmosphere are punctured, while rising sea levels overwhelm the previously secure outlines of islands and continents.

In such a moment, it is understandable that our fantasies turn sclerotic. Tiny infringements produce disproportionate outrage, because everything is at stake; we fixate on the reinforcement of fences, firewalls, valves, dams, checkpoints, tariffs, personal boundaries, restraining orders, visa regimes, customs inspectorates, inoculation procedures, quarantine facilities and so on. Individuals make use of defences once employed only by specialist institutions: surveillance systems, background checks, surgical gloves. They arm themselves against the threat that is *everyone else*, sharpening their own edges, carrying weapons and masks, researching how to identify 'toxic people'.

Yes, it is understandable. But thickened membranes that let nothing through are also fatal. That is why it is so urgent that our response is not to harden, but to reconceive. And the job does not belong to mere governments, lawyers and technology firms. The protections we seek are imaginary and spiritual. Poets and philosophers must show us the way. ■

Rana Dasgupta

TISSUE

Even if you could walk through the corridors
of your body, you would not know which rooms
to enter, which were full of stone. Inside you
there is so much water – a mountain range
in the north to stave off invaders, a desert
in the bacterial colonies of the south. Here
are city buildings, yellowed, without windows,
busy with the making of vaccines and handbags.
Here a double helix strung up the length
of your spine like a flurry of Tibetan prayer flags.
Between these outposts the messengers dart,
carrying tubes of animal hide, pigeons on their backs.
Some ride rams, some travel with consort shadows
in chariots across the skies without once stopping
to look at stars. When they arrive it is almost always
the same. They must remove their sandals and wait
by the mouth of the cave – its fold of skin,
a curtain to trap the wind. They want to tell
you the great fires are still burning, the bees
won't give up their unions, the harvest is both
moon and autumn. You are not alone.

NEWTS

Anita Roy

During its life, a great crested newt will breathe in three distinct ways. For the first four or five months, it is entirely aquatic, breathing through gills that it wears in a froth around its neck like a feather boa. As autumn approaches, the juvenile 'eft' emerges from the water, sheds its gills and begins to breathe with its lungs. It then lives exclusively on land until it reaches sexual maturity at around the age of three, when it returns to its natal pond to spawn. The adult newt is a true amphibian – a creature of both (*amphi*) worlds (*bios*) – slipping easily between the elements, breathing underwater through its skin and above through its mouth.

Like other frogs, toads and salamanders, a newt's skin is a sensitive, receptive and responsive organ, far more open to water- and airborne chemicals than ours. Under a microscope, its skin looks lacy and netted, and it is this very porousness that makes these creatures so vulnerable. To watch a newt hang, arms akimbo, in a column of pond water is to witness a fine balance – its skin is strong and supple enough to hold the creature's shape, yet so delicate that it offers minimal resistance to the cloudy soup of nutrients in which it is suspended. The animal and its surroundings are enmeshed, inseparable parts of a single system.

A third of the world's amphibian species are in imminent danger of extinction. These creatures, like all the rest, are suffering from habitat loss, pollution and climate change. But the amphibians have a specially hellish fourth horseman to contend with: a fungal pathogen called *Batrachochytrium dendrobatidis*, or *Bd* for short.

Bd attacks the keratin in the adult animal's skin, causing chytridiomycosis, or chytrid, a highly infectious disease. A report on its global impact, compiled by no fewer than forty-one scientists from seventeen countries, was published in *Science* in March 2019. It concludes that since the fungus was first identified two decades ago, chytrid has been responsible for the catastrophic decline of 501 known species and the extinction of at least ninety, representing 'the greatest recorded loss of biodiversity attributable to a disease' in history.

Death by chytrid is a slow and cruel affair. As the animal's outer membrane hardens to become an impenetrable barrier, all exchange ceases between the internal organs and the outer world. Osmosis slows and then stops. The circulation of ionic salts grinds to a halt. Oxygen cannot be absorbed nor carbon dioxide expelled. The vital organs shut down – and the animal finally suffocates, hermetically sealed inside its own skin. ■

HOLD YOUR FIRE

Chloe Wilson

.

While waiting for his faecal transplant, my husband wasn't as fun as he used to be. This was largely due to the changes in his diet. He had to be strict. He was down to eating chicken breasts poached in unseasoned water, and a small variety of baby vegetables. Baby carrots, baby corn, baby beets.

'Why only baby vegetables? How is baby corn different from corn?'

I was being peevish. I couldn't help myself.

'It's what the doctor said. I can't take any chances.'

I stared while he cut the piece of baby corn into three, chewing each piece the recommended twenty-five times. I actually counted the movements of his jaw. Twenty-five, right on the money, every time.

I knew that I should take his condition more seriously. The last time Connor had thrown caution to the wind – it was his birthday, he ate a chicken parmigiana and a tiramisu and nearly wept with the joy of it – he'd had to run home from the train station the next morning because, without warning and in considerable volume, he'd shat his pants.

He'd grown wan like a wilting lily on this new diet. It wasn't just the weight loss and the pallor, which left him looking bent, like the weight of his head was too much for his body. It was that he'd lost shape and definition, muscle mass. I felt like I might accidentally skim a bit of him off, the way you can chip part of a mushroom away without really meaning to.

'Anyway. Tell me about your day,' I said, spinning my glass of wine. I'd given up on joining Connor in his misery and was halfway through a bloody steak.

'We went to the park,' Connor said. 'Didn't we?'

Our child, Samuel, nodded enthusiastically. 'Daddy saved a seagull.'

'He did?'

I knew I sounded sarcastic, but Samuel didn't seem to notice.

'It was hurt,' he said.

'I just called the council.' Connor cut his chicken breast along the grain. 'Poor thing couldn't fly. It was the least I could do.'

I could tell he wanted to be congratulated for his humane behaviour, for the good example he was setting.

'They'll just euthanise it, you know,' I said. 'Kinder to let the other birds kill it.'

They would, too. I'd seen the way those gulls went at each other.

Samuel looked at me, appalled. He got up from the table and ran to his father. Connor bent his head to Samuel, and I wished, once again, that Connor wasn't going bald. He looked like a villainous, wispy invalid, especially because his paleness made the rims around his eyes seem a bright watery red, like tomato skins.

Connor put his arm around Samuel and hushed him.

'You said seagull would get better,' Samuel said. Then he commenced whimpering.

This annoyed me. Samuel was a smart child, and he knew where to put a definite article. He reverted to baby talk to soften up my husband. This was unnecessary. If Connor was any softer you'd be able to eat him with a spoon.

'Mummy doesn't mean it,' Connor said, looking over him to meet my eye. 'Mummy's had a hard day at work. She's very tired.'

Mummy was two glasses of wine down and hadn't had satisfactory penetrative sex in over a year.

'Daddy's right,' I said. I drained my glass. 'Mummy's very tired.'

I liked Samuel best when he was asleep, though even then his drooling and the curl of his little marsupial hands irritated me. No one had told me it was possible to dislike your child. Or at least if you did, it was supposed to happen later, when they were bratty teenagers and then ungrateful, smug adults. I didn't like Samuel right off the bat. Don't get me wrong: I loved him – in the sense that I had every intention of discharging my obligations towards him – but, to be frank, he was annoying.

He was fussy, for a start, fussy about temperature and sunlight and noise. He had a series of illogical phobias: he was scared of denim and windshield wipers, and would scream if he could smell bananas. When he danced, he used moves that were weirdly sophisticated, even risqué – rolling his body, thrusting his hips – things he must have dragged up out of the collective unconscious, because he certainly didn't see me or Connor dance like that, or at all. In some ways I was looking forward to the inevitable bullying he'd receive. I was hoping that the cruelty of other children would effect developmental changes that I couldn't seem to trigger.

Worsening all of this was the fact that Connor seemed oblivious. He took no responsibility for his part in creating a defective human being.

One night, in bed, I'd tried to talk to him about it.

'Do you think Samuel's a little . . .'

I was hoping I wouldn't have to finish the sentence.

'A little what?'

I rolled my eyes in the darkness.

'What?' Connor hissed. He still had some grit about him then. He wasn't spending his days on forums, trying to chat up faecal donors.

'You know. You know what I mean.'

'You're talking about our son here.'

'I know that.'

'And there's nothing wrong with him. He's perfect just as he is.'

'Okay, geez,' I said. 'No need to get defensive.'

I rolled over.

Maybe I was able to view things more objectively because I'd thought Samuel was off since he'd been a foetus. He'd felt like an alien in there, wriggling around, eating my lunch, kicking my organs. Connor wouldn't understand. Tapeworms are less intrusive.

It was a relief to get to work in the mornings. I made excuses about having to get in early, about my boss being demanding, but the truth was that my boss was a sanguine paunchy man with a lunch budget of $100,000 per year, who sauntered around humming Ravel's 'Boléro' or selections from the musical *Chess*. My name is Fiona, but he called me Fifi. He had twelve grandchildren and was the one I ended up confiding in about Samuel, about my suspicions that I disliked him as a person.

'Don't worry,' he'd advised. 'You're allowed to have favourites.'

He then told me how he'd ranked his own grandchildren in order of preference. At the top of the list was Maisie, eight, who wore a severe side part and had won the part of Mary in the previous year's Christmas pageant, despite strong campaigning from the parents of two other girls. At the bottom of the list was Eden, five, who had once eaten a bar of soap.

'I mean the whole thing,' Roger said. 'He didn't eat a bit and stop. He ate the whole thing. Was burping bubbles.'

Eden had also dropped his pants in the school playground, unprompted. Roger worried that this might be an indicator of future depravity.

'I've told my son: drive out to the middle of the bush and push him out of the car. He won't listen. Doesn't listen to a word I say.'

He was joking, of course. My office was full of the nicest people I'd ever known. I worked for Raleigh, one of the largest defence, aerospace and security companies in the world. I had studied science and engineering, and had a PhD in mechatronics. I'd spent a number of relatively measly years in the university's engineering department, working on robots or what passed for robots; nothing that was going to pass the Turing test.

It was nice to be where the real money was. At the university, we scrambled and schemed for every grant, every dollar of funding, and

I had to renew my contract every six months. Being an academic felt like being one of those seagulls fighting over the few cold chips thrown by amused tourists. People were only too happy to enter into bitter, decades-long feuds. These fights were often the only thing sustaining their work after the money and accolades dried up.

At Raleigh, though, there were no such problems. There was plenty for everyone and the atmosphere was genial. I'd never known such camaraderie as I found when I started designing missiles for a living.

I was part of the air-to-air missiles team. What we were hoping to achieve was an improved capacity for our missiles to turn around if they missed and passed their target. The problem was a basic one: air-to-air missiles are powered by rocket engines which only burn for a short period of time. Small ones burn for a few seconds, and the larger ones, like AMRAAMs, might have twenty seconds of propulsion.

After that a missile is really a giant dart. And every turn they make – say, in chasing an aircraft which is trying to outmanoeuvre them – creates drag, and drag slows them down, meaning that their target has more chance of slipping away.

Solutions to this problem, or rather ways of mitigating it, already existed. The positioning of the guiding fins, for example. The use of high-altitude attacks, where instead of pursuing the target directly the missile shoots straight up into a less dense altitude, allowing it to go further and lose less speed. It dives when it has run out of fuel and is – hopefully – approaching its target.

But Raleigh thought we could do better. It wanted to develop a missile that could turn in mid-air and fly back at its target with more or less the same speed. It wanted to increase the no-escape zone. This is exactly what it sounds like, and was a selling point when it came to bringing our product to Poland, the UK, Kuwait, Japan, Qatar.

This, however, was a long-term goal. For now we were working on an updated version of our signature AAM, the Raleigh Starling. My team was refining the design and placement of the attitude thrusters that helped guide the missile towards its target. These were tiny, outward-facing rockets which fired when the missile needed to change course. Each could only burn for a fraction of a second. My team was thinking about their angles, their components, their placement.

Roger had no ethical qualms whatsoever about building weapons that could cause massive, instant carnage. I know this because, unprompted, he told me. It was my first week, and I was in our staff kitchen heating up some noodles in the microwave. He was on his way back from lunch. He stuck his head into the room.

'I think your ramen days are over, don't you?'

I looked at the spinning bowl, thought of the invisible waves causing the molecules to go haywire.

'It's good to stay humble. Isn't it?'

He scoffed at this.

'Don't ever be ashamed,' he said. 'Not of the work, the money – none of it. That's what the little people want. To shame you. They don't understand.'

He came close and his voice was low and conspiratorial. Even his halitosis smelled expensive, like beurre blanc and fennel.

'The way I see it,' he said, 'it's like karate. You learn karate so that you never have to use it. And no one looks askance at a man for learning karate, do they?'

I had to agree; they didn't.

'That's the thing you need to remember Fifi,' Roger said, pleased with his own wisdom. 'Everyone holds their fire. It might come down to the last minute, the last second even. But no one really wants to press the button.'

I told Connor about this view of my new position, and he was only too happy to agree.

I'd thought that Connor would disapprove of my working at Raleigh. Weeks earlier, when I told him about the offer I'd received, and how much I'd be paid, he said, 'Sounds great.'

I was surprised. 'Great?'

Connor had briefly been an anarchist, and also a vegetarian. He'd gone through a period of wearing Nehru shirts. Now he was a marketing consultant, but still – I hadn't expected so little resistance.

'Someone's going to do it, right?'

'Sure.'

'May as well be you.'

I had been gearing up for a fight and found myself disappointed I wasn't going to get one.

'You really don't mind?'

He was reading the ingredients on a tub of yoghurt. He didn't answer me. This was just when his digestive problems were turning serious. He peeled the foil lid away from the yoghurt and licked it.

'I have a feeling I'm going to regret this,' he said.

The call came to me because Connor was at an appointment. The appointment was about his faecal transplant, or FMT as he'd taken to calling it. The difficulty he had – the reason he'd been waiting so long – was that FMTs were usually only given to people infected by the stubborn *C. diff* bacteria. People could die from *C. diff* infections, Connor told me during one of his many long stuttering bouts on our en-suite toilet. But faecal transplants were an exceptionally effective treatment. The idea was that the healthy bacteria in the donor stool would wipe out the infection. Rates of success were as high as 95 per cent.

But it wasn't easy to get an FMT if you weren't being treated for *C. diff*. Connor's particularly volatile IBS didn't make him an ideal candidate, and doctors were unwilling or unable – Connor was evasive on this point – to refer him to a colonoscopy centre to have the procedure. That day he was seeing a new doctor, armed with his own research and an email exchange he'd shared with a man he'd met on Poop4You.com. Connor had seen the man's screening results and described his stool as 'pristine'. He'd offered the man $200 for a donation. The man had agreed.

The phone at my desk rang and shocked me out of my reverie. I'd been eating salad and reading an article in *Munitions Journal* about recent constraints in the AAM market. 'Constraints' meant that one war or another had come to an end. Our shares would rise when another one started.

I picked up the phone.

'Fiona Tomlinson.'

'Fiona? Hi, it's Gaby from Blossomings.'

That was the preposterously named early-learning centre that Samuel attended.

'Hello,' I said. I looked at my half-eaten salad and *Munitions Journal* wistfully.

'I'm sorry if this is a bad time. It's just that – well, we have something of a situation.'

'I've told you before. Samuel's not really allergic to bananas, no matter what he says. He's just scared of them.'

'It's not bananas.'

'His sunglasses should be there, if it's the light thing again.'

'No, it's not his photosensitivity. There's been an incident with one of our other pupils.'

This got my attention.

'Oh?'

'I mean, Samuel's okay, he's fine, he's just –'

I let the journal fall closed.

'Just what?'

'I think he should go home for the day. Could you come and collect him?'

'Did someone hurt my son?'

'Mrs Tomlinson –'

'Dr Tomlinson.'

There was a fractional pause.

'*Doctor* Tomlinson. I understand that you might find this an upsetting situation, but I'm here to assure you that at Blossomings, we –'

I hung up and grabbed my keys.

'It's my son,' I said to Roger on the way out. 'He needs to be picked up from day care. Something's happened.'

'Oh God,' said Roger. I started to walk away and my boss's voice followed me down the corridor. 'Did he keep his pants on?'

Blossomings was painted in muted shades that recalled nature: greens and browns, occasional bursts of autumnal orange. It was designed to be at once calming and uplifting. Theirs was an 'expansive' style of education – like a Steiner school, but without the insanity. They let the children play with paint and pipe cleaners, but also introduced them to a few words in Mandarin and taught them to mash their little fists on electric pianos. It was ludicrously expensive, of course, but we were at the point where this gave us relief rather than anxiety; it was good to think that Samuel was surrounded by people who would be influential in the future. He was going to need all the help he could get.

I started heading for Samuel's classroom – his 'Experience Pod' – but Gaby came out and met me in the corridor. Nature sounds – dripping water, breezes through trees, bird calls – floated past us, putting us at ease and allowing us to enter our most creative and receptive states.

'Where is he?'

'Dr Tomlinson, it's so nice to see you. Thank you for coming in. Samuel's fine.'

'Where is he? What happened?'

'Everything's fine.'

'What happened?'

'Why don't you have a seat?'

She gestured to an undulating green bench. I didn't sit.

'So help me God, Gaby, if you don't tell me *right now* what the fuck is going on –'

I was whispering, but pointing, and spittle was flying from my mouth as I enunciated my consonants. My winter coat had cost over $1,000 – it swished in what I liked to think of as an authoritative fashion around my knees. There was a pause, and we heard a kookaburra singing out to signal hunger or distress or desire. Gaby looked around to make sure no one had heard.

'This way,' she said.

Samuel was asleep in the sick bay, or the 'Wellness Centre' as they called it. We stood in a kind of anteroom filled with low children's chairs and educational toys made from felt and wood, and looked in on him through the window like he was in quarantine. There was a Band-Aid on his chin. Blossomings used Band-Aids derived from bamboo.

'If he has any lasting damage –'

'Dr Tomlinson, we can assure you, it's just a little graze. Barely noticeable. He's really here because he needed some space to calm down.'

'He needed to *calm down*? He needed to calm down?'

'What I mean is –'

The door from the corridor opened. We turned to see a frumpy woman coming in, early forties, wearing depressing earth mother-ish clothing – some sort of thermal skivvy stretched over the welcoming expanse of her bosom, a thick elastic headband, a tunic that was probably made from hemp. Her shoes were red and fastened with Velcro. Her leggings had stripes. Her rosacea added another level of clash to the overall ensemble.

'Are you the nurse?' I said. She looked like someone who might work at Blossomings.

'You must be Samuel's mother,' she said, glancing at Gaby. 'Dr Tomlinson – is that right?'

When I assented, she said, 'I hope I'm not interrupting?'

'Oh no, not at all, Deidre,' said Gaby. When Gaby smiled, you could see more gum than tooth. It was off-putting. 'I was just going to come and ask you to join the conversation.'

'Why don't you sit down?' Deidre said to me.

'Who are you?' I said.

Her smile was indulgent. 'Deidre Moss,' she said. 'Luna's mother.'

'Luna?'

'She's in Samuel's pod. They found themselves a little out of sync today.'

'*Out of sync?*'

I was trying to be outraged, but found myself sitting in one of the child-size chairs, my coat's hem limp on the ground, the toes of my pumps pointing at one another. My handbag was in my lap.

Deidre sat too. She reached out and touched my arm. 'They're so mysterious, kids. Aren't they? They have their own little worlds. Who can keep up?'

Deidre was smiling and I could see all the broken veins like little purple lightning forks in her rosacea. I felt like my anger had collapsed in on itself; like I couldn't get it out. I felt like it was making my throat close over.

'Are you feeling okay, Dr Tomlinson?' Deidre asked. She stroked my arm. 'Would you like some water? Gaby, could you be an angel and fetch Dr Tomlinson some water?'

Gaby was only too happy to leave the room. 'Of course,' she said, flashing her gums. 'Take your time.'

Deidre sat back in her chair, using the expanse of her gut as a kind of armrest. 'He's a beautiful little kid,' she said. 'Sammy. Just gorgeous.' No one had ever called him Sammy.

I felt fuzzy headed, like I couldn't remember why we were there. It was those nature sounds. They were getting under my skin. This was why I didn't trust relaxation of any kind.

'Hm,' was all I could manage.

She leaned over. Something she'd applied to her body contained a high percentage of ylang-ylang.

'I've told Connor over and over. Sammy's a gem. Such a funny little kid. Such an original.' She clucked with laughter at a private memory of some amusement my son had afforded her.

Gaby came back in and gave me a biodegradable cup filled with chilled water that had the fluoride filtered out. She wasn't alone. With her was a dour strawberry-blonde child with a downturned mouth and chubby cheeks. I had to admit it; the child was adorable.

'Look who I found!' said Gaby.

'Luna-bear,' said Deidre. The child wandered over with a strange, knowing weariness and flopped her weight into the pillow of her mother's belly. 'There you are.'

The child stared at me.

'I think,' said Gaby, joining us in the circle of tiny chairs, 'now that everyone's here, we ought to talk about what happened today. Just so everyone's feeling okay about it. How does that sound?'

'With the child here?' I said.

'Of course,' said Deidre. 'This concerns her. She should be part of the conversation. Feel free to bring Sammy in. If you're happy for him to be woken up.'

We all gazed into the other room where Samuel slept, untroubled.

Deidre's fingernails were stumpy and cuticles sprang up from their sides. I directed my gaze away from her and towards her daughter.

I looked Luna square in her pale blue eyes. I remembered reading somewhere that the most common eye colour for murderers is pale blue. I wasn't going to let this child intimidate me.

'You're in big trouble,' I said.

'Now just a moment –' said Gaby.

'It's all right,' said Deidre. She held up her hand and Gaby stopped talking. Luna stared up at her. 'Remember what we said about having difficult conversations?'

Luna nodded, though whether she had any comprehension of what Deidre said remained unclear.

'Good girl. Why don't you tell Dr Tomlinson what happened?'

'I punched him,' Luna said then.

'You did *what*?' I hadn't expected her to be so blunt.

'Wait, let's regroup,' Gaby said. 'Remember what you told me, Luna? You said you and Sammy were just playing.'

Luna didn't blink. 'I punched him,' she said again. She stood away from her mother and mimed an uppercut. It was graceful, a sickle-swipe up through the air. 'I punched him like that.'

'And what did he do that made you respond physically?' said Deidre, her voice full of understanding.

'I don't care about her motivations,' I said. I could feel my temper hit a rolling boil. 'She's four. What kind of reason do you expect her to give?'

'She's three, actually,' Deidre said. Luna had returned to her and Deidre was stroking her long, smooth hair. 'Blossomings felt she wasn't being sufficiently challenged in the lower age pod.

She's been accelerated.'

'Uplifted,' Gaby corrected.

'Uplifted,' Deidre repeated. 'Anyway – go on, honey.'

'We were playing goodies and baddies,' said Luna. 'He was the baddy.'

'You see? A simple case of misplaced verisimilitude,' Deidre said. 'She must have read about so-called "goodies" and "baddies" somewhere. I don't allow screen time, obviously, but I don't like to censor her taste in books.'

'Sammy's fine, truly,' Gaby chimed in.

'Samuel,' I said.

'He's the baddy,' Luna said.

'This is fucking ridiculous,' I said, before I could stop myself.

Luna's face was gleeful. 'She said a bad word, Mummy,' she said, her blue eyes on me. 'Is she a bad lady?'

'No, sweetheart,' said Deidre. 'She's just upset. And when people are upset they find it hard to control their feelings.'

Samuel chose that moment to appear at the door. 'Mum?'

'Come here, darling,' I said. 'Let me take a look at you.' He looked wary at my effusiveness, and I didn't blame him. It wasn't exactly my usual mode. But, through loyalty or lack of imagination, he obeyed.

I tilted his chin up, examined his face with its oddly proportioned features that I hoped would grow into some semblance of harmony.

'Do you have a headache?' I asked.

He looked at me hard, trying to figure out the answer I wanted.

'Yes,' he said.

'How many fingers am I holding up?' I held up two. Samuel looked at me, his eyes searching. *Come on*, I thought.

'Four,' he said.

On the way home we stopped at McDonald's. I bought us both ice-cream sundaes with extra chocolate topping.

'Don't tell your father,' I said. He promised he wouldn't. We sat in companionable silence in one of the booths, scratching the sides of our cups with plastic spoons, scraping up every iota of lactose we could get.

In bed that night: another whispered conversation with Connor. I don't know why we whispered; Samuel's room was downstairs. But that was how these talks happened, as though someone were listening, as though they might not approve of what they heard.

'He could have been concussed,' I said.

'But he wasn't.'

'He could have been.'

'He's fine. Aren't you the one who says we should be teaching him resilience?'

'That's exactly what I'm doing. This little bitch came for him and I'm teaching him not to back down.'

'Jesus Christ. She's what – four years old? You really need to let this go.'

I didn't tell him Luna's real age.

'Someone punched our son and you want me to let it go? What the fuck is the matter with you?'

'Nothing. God. I just think you should pick your battles.'

'I do. I pick this one.'

He sighed for dramatic effect in the darkness. I'd demanded that Samuel receive a medical examination, that there be an investigation into Luna's behaviour and Gaby's negligence. I'd felt strangely exalted there in the anteroom, making my list of demands. The rage had been white hot. I'd had the distinct sense that this was how a mother *should* feel; that for once I was getting it right. At home, I'd sent the director of Blossomings a strongly worded email. I wouldn't stop until Luna was expelled from Blossomings. I would make sure she was kept out of every good school. I would hunt down her university applications and see them rejected. I would phone her future employers. I'd show up at her wedding, bristling with objections.

'Try to remember she's just a child,' Connor said.

'Can you grow a spine for a second please? You're supposed to be on my side.'

'I am on your side.'

'Are you in love with Deidre? Is that it? You want to put her floppy tit in your mouth?'

'What? Where did that come from?'

'You want to bury your face in her bush? I bet it's a big one, Connor. I bet it goes all the way to her knees.'

'Christ, Fiona. I wish you could hear yourself sometimes.'

'Have you seen her rosacea?'

'I'm going to sleep.'

R oger, thankfully, was on my side.
'Hippies,' he said, giving a little *humph* of derision. 'It always descends into violence with them, doesn't it?'

We thought we'd come up with an innovative new placement for attitude thrusters, one that might improve their ability to direct the Starling's course. We were waiting for the prototype to be built so that testing could begin. It was a long process and while it was happening Roger was on edge. If we failed, he would be the one answering questions, explaining the budget, justifying our choices.

He was only too happy to have a distraction.

'Tell him to hit her back,' he said.

'I thought of that. But she's a girl.'

'Doesn't really matter at that age. Some girls nowadays are monstrously big. It's the hormones in chicken, they think. All these little overdeveloped girls with huge feet, wearing training bras before they're in primary school – a disgrace, if you ask me. Maisie's chicken intake is supervised very closely. We're thinking of moving her to game birds. Pheasant, quail, that sort of thing.'

We were sitting in his office. He had a whiteboard on the wall with NO ESCAPE ZONE written on it, circled in red. We both wore beautiful suits. His was navy, his shirt blue, his tie white and wet because he'd spilled jus on it at lunch and rinsed it in the bathroom.

'What about insults – has he tried those? Is she fat? Ugly? Stupid?'

'I don't think so.'

'Kids don't have to be PC. If she's slow, or deaf or has an overbite or something he can say it – he's got carte blanche, really. He should take advantage while he can.'

'I've told him to ignore her.'

'Well that never works.'

'I've written a letter to the school.'

He laughed outright at this, a big expulsion of garlic-scented air. 'Goodness me. It's like you want him to be picked on,' he said. 'Seriously, Fifi. Take him aside, and show him how to kick her in the shins.'

Blossomings sent me a very polite and very thorough letter in response to my concerns. They thanked me for taking the time. They remarked upon what a special little boy Samuel was, and how they cherished him, as did his classmates. They said they took my letter very seriously, and after an internal review and lengthy discussions with all involved, had decided that no further action needed to be taken.

I tore the letter up, enjoying the feeling of the heavy, cream recycled stock they used coming apart in my hands.

I wasn't sure what to do next. I supposed I would have to settle for biding my time. Connor, meanwhile, had decided to try being nice to me. He brought me a glass of wine one evening after he'd bathed Samuel and put him to bed. He rubbed my shoulders.

'That's nice,' I said. I leaned my head back against his body, enjoying the pressure of his thumbs against the knots in my shoulders. I'd found part of a parsley stalk between my teeth and was idly grinding it into a pulp.

'God, you're so tense babe,' Connor said. 'You really need to relax.'

Easy for him to say. Due to the IBS, he now mostly worked from home, spending the days in tracksuit pants: a garment that could be quickly lowered and easily laundered.

'I am relaxed.'

'Shh,' he said, 'shhhh.'

I felt my neck lock up. He took my silence for compliance.

'Just breathe,' he said.

Connor never used to say such idiotic things. It was those faecal forums. They were full of people who bought salt lamps and slept with lumps of quartz under their pillows.

'I am breathing.'

'Try counting to five on the inhale.'

'Connor –'

'It really helps.'

I knew he was trying to be nice. *Nice.* The word set my teeth on edge.

'That sort of thing never works for me.'

'You never try it. Come on.'

I realised that my toes in their nylons had actually curled; in distaste, in embarrassment. But I couldn't stand the plea in his voice. With great effort, I did as he asked, breathing in for five counts and out for four.

'There,' he said. 'Don't you feel better?'

I was imagining Luna's uppercut. The unfortunate truth was that I envied her the freedom to make that punch. I imagined it felt wonderful when it connected. I couldn't remember the last time I'd allowed my body to express how I genuinely felt. The stiffness, the tension of keeping myself from doing or saying what I wanted was as close to authentic expression as I was able to get. As I breathed, I imagined my own fist connecting with Deidre's chin.

Inhale.

Exhale.

Inhale.

Exhale.

'You know what?' I said to Connor. 'You were right. I do feel better.'

In the weeks that followed, Samuel reported nothing about Luna. Connor would drop him off, pick him up. I'd get a solemn *ni hao* from him, and the occasional picture made from muddy-coloured pieces of felt. Everyone seemed to have forgotten the entire incident.

I didn't have to go near Blossomings again until Connor went in for his faecal transplant. He had found a specialist centre willing to provide the service for IBS 'on an experimental basis'. Connor was disheartened to learn that he wouldn't be able to select his own donor. The clinic insisted on using their own donors, who were thoroughly screened according to a protocol that Connor perused with reluctant approval. Apparently they dropped off their donations in the morning on the way to work, like chickens delivering their own freshly laid eggs.

'Still,' he said, 'I'd like to know who my donor is. It's personal. They'll become a part of me.'

He said this without a shred of amusement. I made non-committal noises and cracked the top on a bottle of wine.

Connor would be in the FMT centre for half a day. His discharge clashed with the time we needed to pick up Samuel.

That afternoon I looked around in the Blossomings car park, but Deidre and her hefty shoes and ruddy cheeks were nowhere to be seen. Samuel came out, sluggish and wet-lipped as ever. He was swinging his book bag.

'Good day?' I said.

He nodded. He told me he was a wizard and also a dinosaur. I told him that would present certain logistical difficulties.

We drove into traffic. It was drizzly, humid; I could feel my hair frizzing at my temples and smoothed it to no avail.

I cleared my throat and glanced at him in the rear-view mirror.

'How's Luna?' I said.

'Good.'

'Is she a wizard too?'

'No.'

'A dinosaur?'

'She's a fairy.'

I nearly snorted at this. 'Has she hit you again?'

'No.'

'Are you sure?'

A sullen nod, exaggerated, which gave him a momentary double chin. I could see how much he resembled Connor.

'You can tell me if she did. You don't have to lie. I won't be mad.'

'I like Luna,' he said. Then he added, matter-of-factly, 'I'm going to marry her.'

Perhaps some mothers would have laughed, or found this adorable; perhaps that's what Samuel was expecting. I doubt he could have understood the depth of the rage his remark fired in me. All at once I was picturing Luna in a wedding photo on my wall, Luna pushing my red-headed potato-faced grandchild on a creaking swing set, Luna picking over my jewellery as I lay on my deathbed. Luna, breasts wobbling in their training bra, jamming her huge feet into all my beautiful shoes.

The donation didn't work. Or rather, it worked briefly, for a couple of weeks, and then Connor got a little overconfident. He'd begun cautiously, eating a piece of white bread, eating a slice of cheese, eating – to Samuel's horror – a banana. But this moderation didn't last long. Soon Connor was drinking craft beer, eating tubs of choc-chip ice cream, joining me in my glasses of wine and bloody steaks.

'Are you okay?' I asked one night. 'Are you sure?'

He had a forkful of buttery mashed potato.

'Never better,' he said. He pronounced the treatment a miracle. In his most evangelical moments, he proposed writing a book about his experience with FMT in order to raise awareness and diminish stigma. I encouraged him in this, or at least I didn't discourage him. Not because I thought the poop-awareness memoir would ever eventuate, but because he was better with a little iron in his blood, happier, more active. One night he even managed a hopeful erection, which he prodded – its tip oddly cool – into my buttock. It was too fleeting to seize, but still: it gave us hope.

Two days later, however, the run of good times ended. Connor was back in the en suite, squirming and groaning, his feet curled over the footstool he used to make evacuation more comfortable. This had been another recommendation from the forums. Rather than a simple plastic stool that could be purchased anywhere, Connor had invested in an ergonomic timber one: comfortable, warm, but still easy to clean. The forums had a preferred artisan who took Connor's foot size and height into consideration. Connor loved that stool. Whenever we went away for the weekend it came with us in the car.

Connor returned to his diet of poached chicken and baby vegetables, his suspicion of fibre, his hyper-vigilance regarding toxins. Strangely – so strangely I didn't feel I could mention it to him – the smell of his stool, or at least what was left lingering, was different. I didn't realise I had known his smell, but I did, and this wasn't it. This wasn't a stink of ours. This was the stench of an interloper.

Not long after this, Connor called me at work. I declined the call and texted him: I'm in a meeting.

I wasn't in a meeting. I was staring at a page of someone else's equations, looking for errors.

Urgent, Connor wrote.

'For fuck's sake,' I said to no one in particular, and went into the corridor and called him.

'I've just stepped out,' I said when he picked up.

'It's Samuel,' he said.

'Oh Christ.' I made my voice a whisper. 'Did he drop his pants?'

'He – what? No! God, why would you say that?'

'I don't know.'

'No, he's had a fall. He's fine, he's fine, I've picked him up. They wanted us to come in for a conference, but it's fine, I've handled it.'

'A conference?'

'I didn't think it was necessary.'

'What kind of conference?'

'With the school.'

I gave him a moment to provide me with a more complete answer. When he didn't, I said, 'The school? And who else?'

I heard him exhale. 'And Deidre Moss.'

I closed my eyes, felt the fury swirling in my body, saw the inside of my eyelids turn red.

'It's that little cunt of a daughter of hers, isn't it?' I was enjoying myself. 'What the fuck's she done this time?'

Connor's voice was flat.

'He says she pushed him from the top of a slide.'

'You don't believe him?'

'I think it was an accident.' He paused. A long pause. 'You know what he's like.'

I was silent for a second, winded almost. I thought of all the effort I'd put into not only making Samuel, but maintaining his existence. No one, not even Connor, had any concept of the work it took, the exertion, the sacrifice, the tedium, the indignity. How *dare* he?

'Fiona? You there?'

'I'm here.'

My voice was calm.

'I'm sure it was just an accident,' Connor said again. I pictured him rubbing the back of his neck, a self-soothing gesture that never failed to rile me.

'Is that what you're going to say when we're lowering his little casket into the ground?'

I liked the sound of my voice: cool, controlled, an octave deeper.

'Fiona –'

'Better start on that eulogy Connor. Here, let me help. "Today we bury our sort-of beloved son Samuel, and let me say I am so thrilled that Deidre Moss has made the time to be here."'

'For the last time, I'm not in love with Deidre fucking Moss!'

It occurred to me then that I wouldn't care if Connor and Deidre were having an affair. I wouldn't care if Connor was having an affair at all. It would have been like hearing that your teddy bear held parties while you were out.

Connor exhaled heavily. 'Why do you have to see the worst in everything? Why can't you accept that it might have been totally innocent?'

'Don't be so naive.'

'She's a *child*.' He stopped, preparing himself for one of his rare bursts of courage. 'Besides, can't you let me handle this? Can't you support me in anything? You're supposed to be my wife!'

I laughed at this. I could see Roger coming back from lunch, smelling of something rich and beefy. We smiled and waved at one another.

'Don't be ridiculous,' I said. 'If anything, you're my wife.'

I hung up.

I called Blossomings and said yes, we would like to have a conference. It was to be held after hours in the office of Blossomings' director. We left Samuel in a supervised play area, taking two long yellow building bricks and directing them gently and pointlessly at one another.

The director was a woman wearing what looked like a very deluxe poncho; some kind of violet cashmere. Her hair was in a pixie cut, her eyeshadow a sheeny pale-pink champagne, her blush apricot. She looked like the thick-waisted but winsome model who would appear in a magazine next to the words FABULOUS AT ANY AGE.

'Mr Tomlinson, Dr Tomlinson, won't you come in,' she said, indicating two chairs upholstered in green felt. There was a salt lamp in the room.

'Are you expelling her?' I said. I saw no reason to put myself through niceties.

Ms Simon – she pronounced it 'Simone' – said, 'Would you like a liquorice tea?'

'I would like,' I began, 'for my son to graduate preschool without permanent spinal trauma.'

She smiled at Gaby, who was also in the room. 'Some tea, Gaby? Thank you so much.'

When the door closed she sighed a long, luxurious sigh. I wondered if she was counting to four.

'Samuel is such a –'

There was a knock.

'Such a?' said Connor, his face hopeful. 'Such a what?'

I shot him a look which he didn't acknowledge. Ms Simon ignored him and called, 'Yes?'

Deidre was wearing her most sombre pinafore; charcoal with red buttons at the shoulders. She wore black boots that looked like part of a wetsuit. I figured this was her way of acknowledging the gravity of the situation.

The discussion did not proceed smoothly. Deidre said it was an accident; I put it to her that her child was a sociopath. Ms Simon nodded gravely. Eventually, after we'd been circling each other for fifteen minutes, Ms Simon said, 'I think we should bring the children in.'

They entered with their usual attitudes: Samuel's wide-eyed trepidation, Luna's thuggish nonchalance.

Ms Simon put a twinkle in her eye when she addressed the children. I wanted to tell Samuel that it was a trap, that all charm is a trap, but it was too late – he was already mesmerised, sitting on the child-sized chairs that Gaby had added to the semicircle on our side of the desk, sticking as many knuckles in his mouth as he could fit, staring at Ms Simon the way that a village idiot would stare at the risen body of Christ.

'Now,' Ms Simon said, 'the first thing I want to say is that no one here is in any trouble. All right? We just want you to tell us everything that happened. Samuel, why don't you go first?'

Something a cop would say. I wanted to tell Samuel not to say anything incriminating, or stupid. Connor put his hand on my thigh. I realised I had almost launched out of my seat.

Samuel kept his mesmerised gaze on Ms Simon, locked on her, and I could see how she enjoyed this, see the bullet point on her executive-level resume: *Key Skill: Excellence in establishing rapport.*

'Luna pushed me,' Samuel said. He said it all in a rush, like it escaped from him, like it pained him to admit it. Ms Simon smiled.

Luna tried to interrupt. 'No I didn't!' she began. 'I didn't! I –'

Ms Simon's smile was calm and immovable. 'Luna, you'll have your turn in just a moment.' She turned back to Samuel.

'When did she push you?'

'I was waiting my turn for slide.'

'Were the two of you talking? Do you know why she pushed you?'

Tears appeared in his eyes. He shook his head.

'Don't know,' he said. 'Don't know.'

Then he stared crying in earnest. It was embarrassing how openly he wailed. Connor was the one who went to him, made him blow his nose – which he did with great zeal and limited accuracy – and made the requisite murmuring noises.

'Luna?' said Ms Simon. 'What do you remember?'

I almost smirked. It was impossible to prove a negative. Good luck, kid, I thought. It was only then, realising that she wasn't answering the question, that I really focused on Luna's broad face. Her brows were tilted in confusion. Her cheeks were bright red. Her eyes were wet, though she didn't cry. She looked at her mother and her terror was real.

I saw that she was telling the truth.

'I didn't,' she said, finally, her chest heaving with her rapid breaths. Wow, I thought. She really is a child. She seemed fragile, unformed; I suddenly sensed the weight of my advantage over her.

She started shaking her head. 'He's lying!' she said. She even did a dramatic courtroom point at my sobbing son, who by now had saturated the shoulder of Connor's shirt with his various secretions.

Deidre weighed in.

'Ms Simon,' she said, adding a slight French accent to the name, as though this would buy her extra points for accuracy, for attention to detail. 'They're little kids. Who knows what happened. It's his word versus hers. I think we should just draw a line under this and move on.'

She sat back, hands linked primly on her gut.

Ms Simon gave her a look filled with great concern.

'My worry is that this is becoming a pattern of behaviour with Luna,' she said, smiling when she said the child's name, as though Luna were a dog who would understand only that word and none of the others.

'What I propose, and what I hope all parties will agree is for the best, is that both children attend counselling; Samuel for his trauma, Luna for her tendency towards finding a physical outlet for her aggression. I suggest we also have Luna sign a behavioural contract, in which she promises never to touch another child without their consent. How does that sound?'

Her voice was like butter.

Luna started pulling on Deidre's pinafore. 'Mum, I didn't do it,' she said. 'I didn't!' Her voice was desperate.

Deidre laid a comforting hand on the top of her child's head.

'I'm not sending her to counselling for something she didn't do,' said Deidre, smiling, looking around, hoping to find support in the room. 'She's only three. There's been some confusion. That's all.'

'I understand this must be difficult,' said Ms Simon. 'However, while we cherish all our pupils at Blossomings, safety must be paramount. I'm afraid these are the conditions of Luna's return to learning. If they don't suit your needs, I will completely understand if you would like to enrol her elsewhere.'

Deidre took a moment to comb her fingers through Luna's beautiful strawberry-blonde hair. The child clung to her mother, staring at me, at Connor, at Samuel with genuine fear and genuine hatred. The expression on her mother's face showed, in a less raw manner, that she felt the same way.

She swallowed and it was audible.

'I think I see what's happening here,' she said. Her voice was trembling. 'This little snake of a child' – here she looked at Samuel, who was still snivelling – 'has invented a story to get my daughter into trouble. He's gone so far as to throw himself off the equipment, and because you're so scared of a fucking lawsuit –'

'Language,' I said, not quite under my breath.

Deidre turned her shrewd gaze to me. 'Oh piss off,' she said. 'Do you think I don't know who you are? What you do? Do you know?' she said, addressing Ms Simon. 'This woman makes bombs. She literally makes fucking weapons that blow little kids like these sky-high.'

I wondered how she knew that. Was she obsessed with me? Had she been googling my name deep into the night, reading the corporate profile that popped up on Raleigh's website?

'Deidre, I am going to have to ask you to be mindful of your language,' said Ms Simon.

'Seriously?' Deidre spat. 'That's what you care about? Here we are because one child fell – deliberately, I might add – a few feet onto a safety mat. She's out there dreaming up ways to blow thousands of kids to kingdom come and you honestly don't give a shit?'

Connor chose this moment to speak. 'It's not like that,' he said, his voice firm. 'It's like karate.'

Ms Simon drew the meeting to a close.

We drove home in companionable silence. Samuel slept in the back seat. That night the domestic things happened in quiet harmony; Connor and I were gracious with each other, feeding and bathing Samuel, setting the table, pouring wine, stacking the dishwasher. That night, the cool tip of Connor's enquiries at my hip; and though it didn't quite happen, it almost did.

It was a week or so later that I had the idea that Samuel would make an ideal donor for Connor. He had no parasites, no history of sexually transmitted diseases; he hadn't had time to develop a dependency on alcohol or drugs. Connor had read about DIY faecal transplants, but had thought it was too risky to try. He wanted the doctor, the twilight anaesthetic, the certainty that the donation would be sprayed all the way up to the top of his bowels. I convinced him to try it my way.

I watched an instructional video and let Samuel watch it with me. In it, a man demonstrated how to make the solution. He did this by putting a chocolate-coated banana into a blender with water and salt. I thought Samuel would be horrified at the sight of the banana, but he just watched, fixated, as the mixture whizzed to the consistency of a milkshake.

The next day, I explained to Samuel that he had to pass his stool into a sterile plastic container because his donation was very precious. This explanation was good enough for him; he nodded, sombre as a bishop. I let him stay in the kitchen while I used the blender to mix his donation with saline solution and draw it into an enema bulb. Afterwards, the blender went straight into the rubbish bin outside.

I didn't allow Samuel to watch the next part. I barely wanted to see it myself. Connor and I locked ourselves in the en suite. I laid garbage bags on the floor, and handed Connor a pillow wrapped in a garbage bag that he could rest on while the enema took effect. I wore gloves, and a mask, and I tried to be gentle as I parted my husband's buttocks and saw the thick, pasted-down whorls of hair in there, and the aperture at their centre.

'It's all right,' Connor said, when he thought I wasn't applying sufficient pressure. 'It doesn't hurt.'

I prodded harder; then I squeezed as hard as I could. When the bulb was empty I sat with him for the requisite time the websites told us to wait before he could empty his bowels. Connor lay on the pillow, naked and groaning. When the timer went off, I left the room.

'What do you think?' I asked when he emerged, still unsteady, from the shower. 'Do you think it worked?'

His smile was like weak tea. 'I feel better already,' he said.

Samuel was glad to hear how much he'd helped. I never asked him about Luna again; I didn't need to. She undertook the counselling and came back to Blossomings, and if she was seething with anger, anger that would last the rest of her miserable life, that wasn't my problem.

Besides, there was nothing to ask. I already knew the truth. I knew what I'd seen in Luna's face. But I was not appalled at my son. Later, I'd go for walks with him and Connor, and watch him surrounded by cranky, grasping gulls. I'd watch how he tempted them with a soggy chip and then chased them all away, giving them nothing. In a moment they'd come back, gathering around him, their eyes on the morsel he held. Their violence, their displeasure, was all directed at one another.

The game delighted him. He smiled at me and I smiled back, finally feeling it, that glow of love I was supposed to have for my own flesh and blood.

Ah, my little starling. He wouldn't be the kind of person who seemed particularly talented, or beautiful, or charming, or forceful. He might not leave much of an impression at all. But when the time came – and it always came, always – he would be the one to push the button. ■

LAXMI

Anita Khemka

Introduction by Rana Dasgupta

A few doors away from where Anita Khemka grew up in Delhi lived a band of big, sari-clad women with facial hair and deep voices. Whenever she was naughty, her grandmother issued a threat that was terrifying to the young girl: 'If you don't behave yourself, I'll send you to live with the hijras.'

Many years later, Anita went to live with the hijras of her own accord. 'I use my camera to deal with my fears,' she says. 'I photograph when I feel a compelling need, usually when something disturbs me.'

That was when she met Laxmi.

The first son of a Hindu Brahmin family, Laxmi Narayan Tripathi felt neither male nor female. She joined a hijra community, so adopting South Asia's 'third sex', which embraces eunuchs, intersex and transgender people. For centuries, hijras have lived on the fringes of society in closed communities run by powerful leaders called gurus.

While working on a documentary about the hijra community, Anita learned about Laxmi's childhood experiences of abuse: that she had been raped by several of the men in her family, and what a huge impact these events had had on her sexuality. 'That's when we first bonded,' Anita remembers. 'It took us a few years to start trusting each other.'

From a young age Laxmi had an aptitude for dance, and dedicated herself to the art as a way of coping with her trauma. Traditionally, hijras dance and dispense blessings in the houses of newborn children, for which they often receive substantial offerings of money, and as an accomplished dancer Laxmi fitted well into this role. She had no interest, however, in the other trades to which contemporary hijras are usually subjected: begging and sex work. Charming and articulate, she had a social vision and knew how to make connections. Anita witnessed the rise of Laxmi's public profile; over the years Laxmi was invited to HIV conferences and transgender film festivals. She began to travel all over the world. She became a figurehead for hijras and sex workers, including with the UN.

Anita's documentation of Laxmi developed into what has become a lifelong friendship bound by photography. 'Sometimes I am with her and don't feel like photographing her at all, and she says – because she's a diva – "See how amazing I look right now, with the light falling at this angle. I am giving you an incredible shot. Pick up your camera."'

Laxmi remained biologically male, but she had her breasts surgically enlarged. Her critics called her a *bahrupiya*: 'shape-shifter' or, more vindictively, 'impostor'. Anita recalls, 'She told me she would never wish to be castrated – the hijras say "reach nirvana" – as that would mean a final crossover of sorts.' The ritual removal of the penis and testicles is commonly part of a hijra's initiation into the community, but for many years Laxmi resisted. After all, she was the eldest son of a Hindu Brahmin family. She was still negotiating her place within her community and society at large.

She became a spiritual leader and acquired a following. An Indian Supreme Court judge requested an audience with her. He came to see her for three days in a row, and each time she turned him down. On the fourth day, she received him, and he entered with a young woman. 'Your daughter is unable to bear children,' observed Laxmi. 'How did you know?' asked the judge. 'Within a year, she will have a child,' said Laxmi. 'When that happens, bring me bangles of gold.' Everything happened as she predicted.

Laxmi's religious aura is exceptional among hijras, who do not usually reach deity status. They thrive on being ambiguous and in general, people are fearful of being cursed by them. And just as much as people believe they can be cursed by a hijra, people in turn believe in the power of their blessing.

Hijras of all religions usually embrace Islam, which is traditionally sympathetic to their subculture, and Laxmi loved to visit Muslim shrines. She became involved with a Muslim man. Aryan, who had been born female but identified as male, had undergone sex reassignment surgery and was now a well-known bodybuilder. In 2019 they were engaged at Mahakaleshwar Jyotirlinga temple, Ujjain.

But Laxmi's public life was becoming more entwined with Hindu nationalism. At last year's Kumbh Mela, she paraded with the swords and tridents beloved of the ideological movement's militant wing. She courted the ruling Bharatiya Janata Party, whose antipathy to India's Muslims is well known. She moved to the capital city of Delhi in the hope of entering politics.

She came under attack. Many of her followers resented her alliance with the far-right governing party. They began to reject her leadership, saying, 'Laxmi speaks for hijras, but she is still a man. She is still keeping her options open.' In 2019, Laxmi found herself in a very different situation to when she first entered the hijra community. Eventually, she decided to attain nirvana.

The rituals surrounding castration borrow from those of marriage and childbirth. After the operation, there is complete seclusion for forty days. Then, like a bride on the eve of her wedding, the new eunuch is scrubbed with yellow turmeric, bathed and dressed in green clothes, a colour that symbolises fertility. She emerges from the house to dispose of her old clothes in the river. An evening of dancing and festivity ensues.

Laxmi now finally finds her soul in sync with her physical body. As her friend and confidante, Anita will stay close. 'We both know that I will continue photographing her until one of us dies,' says Anita. 'She is as much invested in this document as I am.' ∎

SELF

And when they ask, what kind of animal
would you be, I always say gazelle or lark,
never cockroach, even though they'll outlast
us all. Once I dreamed I had a body with two
heads like those ancient figures from the Zarqa
River – bitumen eyes, trunks of reed and hydrated
lime, built thick and flat without genitals, nothing
shameful to eject except tears. We all want to be
monuments but can't help shoving our fingers
in dirt. Imagine a life in childhood – one face
to the womb, another to the future. What we remember
is the road, peering through a lattice at dusk,
the trauma of burial. Will we have terracotta
armies to take us through, will we be alone
with the maggots? How good the rain is
after a failed romance. Never mind the muddy
bloomers. We are appalled by life and still,
any chance we get we emerge from the earth
like cicadas to sing and fuck for a moment
of triumph. The shock we carry is that the world
doesn't need us. Even so, we go collecting parts –
an afternoon by the sea, a game of hopping on
and off scales, nose low to the ground, looking
for that other glove to complete us.
Here I am globe, spinning planet.
Tell me why are you not astonished?

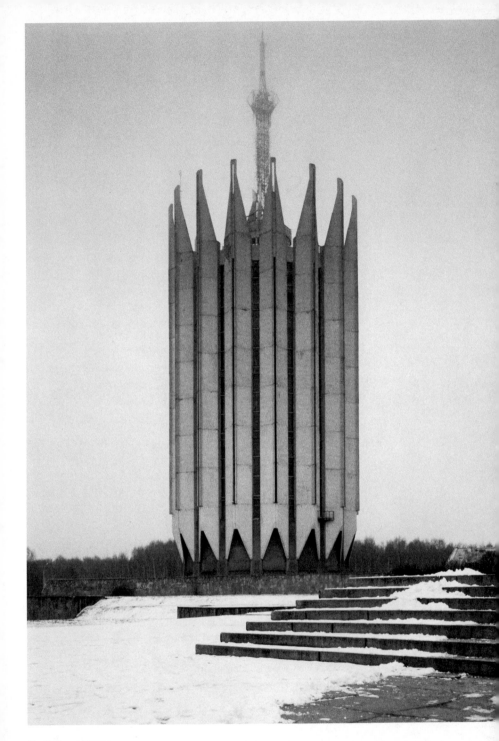

Institute of Robotics and Technical Cybernetics, St Petersburg, 2006

THE STATION

J. Robert Lennon

The air was cold, the waves were choppy, and a bright, gray fog surrounded the boat, impenetrable as a darkness. It was seven thirty in the morning, and I had no idea where in the world I was.

Everything I needed would be provided on the island, they'd told me. All I should bring was three days' worth of underclothes to complement my uniform, which I was assured I could launder on-site. They also recommended coat, hat, gloves and boots: the island could make even the most clement weather feel autumnal.

The nameless officer who briefed me just called it the Station. When I asked him to show me the location on a map, his jaw twitched. 'We had it removed,' he told me. I supposed the intention was to prevent me from blabbing to family and friends. If so, he needn't have worried – I had none close enough to confide in. And as far as I could tell, the boat might as well have been trawling in circles for the past ninety minutes. Maybe this was all a joke – some elaborate test. Maybe I'd be deposited back at the base, congratulated for passing muster and given my real assignment – some desk job on the mainland, or foreign bureaucratic posting. For a moment, thinking about it, I hoped this would be the case. I didn't exactly regret accepting the post – a bit of solitude, I thought, would do me good. But the cold and fog had seeped under my collar and into my head, and I longed, unexpectedly, for the comforts – however meager – of home.

I wasn't to wonder about these matters for long. For the last five minutes, I'd been standing on the port side of the boat, my gloved hands gripping the gunwale, trying to descry something, anything, through the curtain of fog. Now, suddenly, the undifferentiated gray gave way to shapes: wisps and tendrils, eddying and parting, agitated in our wake. The engine moaned, the vessel lurched beneath me, and suddenly I could see green, emerging first in a ragged, distant patch, and then, as the fog dispersed, all at once; and the island exposed itself to us, like a pervert unveiling his tumescence from behind an old colorless raincoat.

It really did appear pornographic at first, after the demure and shapeless gray of the fog: a massive crag, thrusting into the dead sky, black rock smeared in moss and bird shit. Then we drew closer and lurched starboard – I nearly lost my grip on the railing – and the rest of the island shrugged into view. It was a C-shape, roughly, variegated gray along the shoreline, grass-green above that, then the moss and dung and black peak. Two black peaks, I saw now, at opposite ends of the landmass. They were connected by a rounded spine, a thing I imagined you could climb up to and walk along.

The place had once been occupied. Several rows of abandoned stone cottages formed a small village on the plain; their roofs, doubtless thatch from the mainland, had long ago rotted away. To the north, a squat concrete block had been sunk into a hillside. Behind it, three enormous radio masts reached up to disappear into the clouds; each was as thick at the base as a giant redwood, and sprouted a motorized antenna array whose leaves silently pivoted as I watched. Together the towers evoked an executive board or panel of judges: stoic, watchful. Along with the concrete bunker, they doubtless comprised the Station.

The boat pulled up alongside a small pier, sturdily constructed of reinforced steel plates bolted to concrete pilings. The captain climbed out, tied up and turned to face me, his large eyes squinting out from under a damp canvas hood. I could detect, beneath his red beard, a tight, irked mouth; it said, 'Well, get off.'

I shouldered my bag and climbed up onto the pier. It was heavy, well anchored and made little noise under my feet.

The captain towered over me. 'I'll be here for an hour,' he said. 'If he misses me, I won't be back for a week.'

'I'm sorry,' I said. 'Misses you? Who?'

In response, the captain just thrust his chin towards my presumptive HQ. 'Him. Move him along.'

The wind was strong at my back as I trudged up the rocky beach to the path that led through the old village. The cottages were ghostly, colorless. The wind roared through them, making strange music out of their empty windows and doorways. Inside some of them, the remains of wooden tables and chairs lay decaying on the dirt floors. A few tin cans, a fork or spoon. At the threshold of one cottage, a word had been chiseled into an irregular flagstone: VILCOEM.

Soon I'd passed the village and begun the climb up to the Station. It took longer than I expected – distances were deceptive here. Eventually I arrived at a featureless steel door, its paint worn away by the weather. A hinged plastic housing concealed a large recessed button that glowed green. I pressed it.

Nothing happened for a long time. I watched a lone gull ride an updraft and settle on one of the towers. Just as I was about to buzz again, a series of clanks issued from the door and it fell slowly open.

If I'd expected to be greeted cheerfully, or at all, I was to be disappointed. By the time the door had opened far enough to allow entry, my predecessor had already turned his back. He was scurrying down a long hallway illuminated by dim yellow bulbs dangling from green metal shades. As I watched, he ducked through an open door, and I heard him in there, stomping about and banging drawers shut. I closed the door behind me and looked around.

I was standing in a large storage area. Boxes of food, toiletries and cleaning supplies were stacked to the ceiling along all the walls. A pair of work boots lay on a rubber mat just beside the door. They were like my own, brown leather affixed to thick crêpe soles, except heavily scuffed and worn.

A grunt echoed down the hall behind me, and I turned. He was around my age and height, though thinner, and he wore the same casual duty uniform, though somewhat worse for wear. A duffel, also the same issue as mine, was slung over his right shoulder. His dark hair was messy and much longer than men like us typically maintained it. But the most noteworthy thing about him was his beard: thick, long, it covered his lower face and neck entirely, and had crept up over much of his cheeks as well, sparing only enough room for two tired eyes, which gazed at me in apparent fascination.

'Fucking hell,' he said. His voice was gruff, precise and a bit nasal.

I said, 'The captain wants you to hurry.'

The man laughed – dismissively, I thought, as though I'd just said something irritatingly obvious.

He was tying his boots the same way I did: laced two eyelets shy of the top, and double-knotted. As his hands moved, I experienced a sense of déjà vu, as though I'd been here before, and watched this man tie his shoes. He stood up and reached for the door latch. 'Excuse me,' he said. 'I have a boat to catch.'

'Wait!' I said. 'What am I – that is –'

'Manual's on the desk in the bedroom. When it says every three hours, it means every three hours.' He punctuated these words by poking my chest with a trembling finger. 'Also –'

'What?'

He shook his head. 'Never mind. It's pointless. You'll do it anyway.' He flung the door open and tramped out into the wind. The clouds were parting, and the sun was visible just over the ridge. Soon it would descend, and my side of the island would be cloaked in shadow.

I followed him a few steps down the slope. 'Tell me!' I shouted. 'I want to get it right.'

He shook his head, stared briefly at the ground. Then he looked up, pointed at me, and said, 'You're gonna want to go down the other side of the mountain and check out the Facility. Don't do it. Okay?'

'Facility?'

'Unbelievable,' the man said. 'There you go. I can hear it in your voice.'

'Hear what?'

A horn cut through the damp. The man raised his arm and waved. The air was clear enough now to make the captain out, leaning out of the bridge and waving an arm back. My predecessor set off, walking backwards. Then he turned and ran, full tilt, down the grassy slope towards the pier.

I carried my bag into my quarters. A bed, a dresser, a desk. A clothing rack, in lieu of a closet. The bed had been stripped and the dirty linens lay in a ball on the floor. Tsking, I dropped my bag, grabbed up the greasy sheets and set off in search of the laundry room. I found it at the end of the hall, next to a bathroom that contained a small shower, sink and toilet. I stuffed the sheets into the washer, grabbed down some detergent from a shelf and set the machine churning. Then I walked back down the hall and peered into the room where I would be doing my work.

The control room was drab and imposing, with pale green painted cinderblock walls and a gray linoleum floor. A long, thin window stretched across the back wall and looked out onto the mossy face of the north hill. At this hour, it let in some meager light that, along with the room's dim incandescence, illuminated a heavy console of switches, dials and gauges. This console had been installed along three walls of the room, and was dominated, in the center, by an extraordinary visual display.

Approximately four by six feet, this object resembled an oil painting more than it did an electronic device. In fact, that's what I thought it was, at first, a painting, of the island itself and the surrounding ocean as seen from above, complete with the cottage rows, the towers, the dock and the building I was now standing inside. Then I noticed a faint shimmer in the water and, moving closer, realized that all of it, the entire image, was in slow, undulating motion. I was not looking at a static depiction. Rather, it was a constantly updating likeness, a live feed, rendered in three dimensions – as though the textured surface of a paper globe had come to life. I leaned closer, nearly touching my nose to the rippling surface, until I could make out an incalculable quantity of tiny shafts, each glowing, shifting in color, moving infinitesimally in and out with the movement of the waves. I was wondering how such a thing was possible when I realized that I could hear them as well: the whir of the tiny motors that powered each pinlike element, accompanied by the hum, like a distant insectile swarm, of whatever technology caused the shafts to fluctuate, ever so subtly, in position, color and luminance.

On the work surface beneath the display lay a leather-bound ledger, where my predecessor had been logging, in pencil, readouts from the control panel and the adjustments he had made, via the various knobs and levers, to maintain these at their proper values. He'd marked the time for each of the readouts and they were indeed taken every three hours, on the hour. I remembered what he'd said as he headed for the boat and scanned the ledger for the last entry. In a sudden panic I glanced at my watch: I had only seven minutes before the next readouts were due.

I ran to the bedroom and picked up the manual he had left behind. He was right: the procedure was indeed very clear. I didn't have many responsibilities here except to keep my body healthy and to maintain this system. I hurried back to the control room, lay the manual open on the desk, and followed the instructions as quickly as possible: recording the values indicated by each readout; adjusting the knobs, levers and switches to nudge those values into the proper range; and taking note of the new values. The only remaining task was to enter all the new data into the terminal.

I almost made it. I was just sitting down before the terminal's keypad when a piercing ring issued from a faceless telephone hanging on the wall above it. I answered with my name, title and personnel code, as was customary, and a woman's voice replied, 'The figures are late.'

'I'm sorry. I'm entering them now.'

'They are to be entered every three hours, on the hour, except in cases of high alert, during which time they must be entered every half-hour, on the half-hour, without exception.'

'I know. It's my first day,' I explained. 'My first hour, in fact.'

'You'll be permitted two further irregularities, at which time your assignment will fall under judicial review. If found negligent, you could be suspended, terminated or imprisoned.'

Imprisoned? No one had informed me of that possibility. 'I understand. There,' I said, clicking the SUBMIT key. 'It's done.'

During the pause that followed, I could hear the sounds of a busy command center. I wondered where the woman was. She said, 'Data received. Under the provisions outlined in the manual of conduct, section 3, item 14a, you have received your first of three warnings. Do you acknowledge?'

'Sure.'

'The permissible responses are yes and no, sir.'

'Yes.'

'Thank you. Good evening.'

I intended to explore my surroundings, but there wasn't much to explore. A cramped exercise room, complete with a treadmill and some barbells. A bookcase in the foyer filled with adventure, horror and western paperbacks. I ate food from cans and drank water from bottles and listened, briefly, to a radio broadcast in a language I didn't understand. I slept surprisingly deeply between midnight and my 3 a.m. monitoring session, and after my 6 a.m. session, enjoyed a few brief sorties, on foot, around the east side of the island, as the towers' ambient hum mingled with the sound of the rushing wind.

I experienced a brief panic in the control room when I noticed, upon arriving, a small dark spot on the gravelly verge outside the headquarters, moving towards the door. Alarmed, I dashed out and looked around. Nothing. When I returned to the monitor, the spot was gone – but then it reappeared for a moment before moving, once again, towards the door. The spot was me. The display, it seemed, had a latency of about ten seconds.

Another night passed before I decided to climb to the lowest point on the ridge and see the east side of the island for myself. I knew from the control-room display that there wasn't anything there: a steep declivity of bare rock, probably impossible to walk down, terminating in violent seas. But I wanted a look, before settling in to what would doubtless prove a long, dull relationship with the Station's collection of paperbacks. I waited until just after my 3 p.m. data upload, when the grass was at its most dry, laced up my boots and made a beeline for a small notch in the ridge, just southeast of HQ. I walked at a good clip and maintained my speed as the climb got steeper. I noticed that the grass had been trampled, creating a sort of path up to the notch. Animals might have created it, but so far I'd seen no animal life at all, save for the seabirds and a few insects. The only reasonable conclusion was that my predecessor had walked this same route – perhaps quite often, in fact.

All told, it took me about twenty minutes to reach the top, accompanied by the sough of the wind against the rock, the rasp of my boots through the grasses, my labored breathing and the distant, unanswered cry of a bird, somewhere beyond my vision. When I arrived, I was startled by what lay before me: the ocean, yes, churning against the craggy black of the unforgiving shore that the control-room display had shown me; and, at my feet, the softly humped green ridge that led north and south to the island's two peaks. But the steep wall of rock between the two was interrupted by a long, low, gray structure situated just above the beach and extending an indeterminate depth into the hillside itself. Its placement would seem, from an engineering perspective, to be foolish in the extreme; the blasting, materials delivery and man-hours expended in such an unforgiving location must all have been extraordinarily costly. Yet there the building sat, seemingly as monolithic and unchanging as the rock itself, as though it had been there for a century. Indeed, it was almost as though the building had existed first and the mountain had grown over it, like a tree does through a chain-link fence.

My predecessor had told me this place existed – the Facility. Gazing at it from the ridge, I experienced a strange kind of vertigo: a sensation that my mind, not my body, might tumble down the cliff side, be dashed against the structure's brutal corners and surfaces. This feeling ought to have terrified me. Instead it manifested as an urge, a hunger to be broken.

I took a step back. I'd want to climb down and explore, my predecessor had told me, and I should resist the temptation. He'd also dismissed, in the same breath, the possibility that I might actually resist. I did want to explore, of course, but I also wanted to prove him wrong. On the other hand, I wanted to defy him, which, quixotically, I could accomplish by proving him right.

My plans were further complicated by the dampness of the air and the slipperiness of the rock. My boots were made to grip surfaces like this, but there was only so much they could do on a slick, sheer plane. A good fifty yards separated me from the structure below, plenty of room to take a wrong step and fall to my immediate – or worse, slow and agonizing – death. How long would my body lie there before anyone was sent to investigate? Days, perhaps. And by then I might not only be dead, but torn asunder by the waves, or scavenged by birds and fish, carried away in tiny pieces high into the sky and deep into the sea. There wouldn't even be remains to ship back to the mainland, or even evidence of what had happened to me. By all appearances, I would have simply disappeared – ceased to exist.

I turned around and began the walk back down the hill.

For several days, I found it fairly easy to keep myself occupied. I began an exercise regimen involving the small workout area of the Station and frequent brisk walks around the west side of the island. I tried, once, to circumnavigate the entire island by walking along the beach, but the peaks defeated me: their steep flanks plunged directly into the water, cutting off any possibility of safe traversal. Several times a day I passed through the village and tried to imagine the people who had once lived there. Sheep herders, I suspected, based upon the startling cairn of bones I encountered in a small cave near the northern end of the beach. What must it have been like to grow up in such a place? Perhaps living here sharpened the imagination and toughened the body. Or not – perhaps they went mad from loneliness.

My own childhood had been spent largely alone, which is part of what made me a good candidate for this assignment. I began to work my way through the bookcase, starting with the westerns. Some of them seemed familiar to me, and I wondered if these specific titles might have been among the ones I had stashed in my dusty corner of the attic, where I would quietly read, hiding from my father, when I was supposed to be out playing baseball or riding my bike. There in the Station, as I read, I remembered the sound of my parents' arguments, my mother's crying fits, my father's dialogue with the television, which they didn't realize I could hear.

I was dimly aware that summer would soon come to an end, and that I should capitalize on the good weather by toning my mind and body for winter. So I continued to take walks up on the ridge, and occasionally would gaze down at the Facility, wondering who had occupied it and why, and how they had got there. I could see no dock on the beach below. It was conceivable that a helicopter might be able to land on the roof – but of course nothing of the sort had happened during the weeks I'd resided here.

One sunny afternoon, when the grass was dry and the earth was hard, I found myself standing on the ridge once again, staring at the sheer rock face below. I was startled to realize that, in spite of myself, I was tracing a possible route down to the Facility. I could make out obvious footholds on the rocks – a series of serendipitous stairs, almost as regular as if they were man-made. And then, after further observation, I decided that they actually were man-made – cleverly hewn out of the existing rock for the very purpose of reaching the Facility below from the lowest point on the grassy ridge. Irregular they were, yes, but operational.

And the more I thought about my predecessor's warning and dismissal, the more I believed that he himself had probably climbed down there as well. His sneering contempt wasn't directed at me – a man he'd never met – but at himself, for betraying a nonexistent 'rule' that for some reason he believed was important.

Why should I permit my own behavior to be dictated by a stranger's obscure system of values? There was nothing in the manual that forbad exploration of the western shore of the island, and I had two and a half hours to go before my next upload.

At first, the going was less perilous than I'd imagined. Whoever had made these steps had taken great care with them, maintaining a reasonably uniform height for each and angling them to accommodate the folds of rock. I descended the first twenty yards swiftly, and the Facility gradually rose to meet me.

But at some point I must have made a wrong move. A shallow ledge appeared to lead to a lower one, and one lower than that – but several steps down I realized that I was no longer treading on man-made cuts. What looked like a stair revealed itself as a steeply canted surface, and my feet flew out from under me. Hands grabbing at empty air, I fell, and my chin met the rock in an explosion of pain. For a moment I was certain I would go sliding to my death, but I managed to curl my fingers into a declivity, and my feet found purchase on a small outcropping. I hugged the mountainside, gasping, and could see, just ten feet to my left, the path I should have taken – my mistake was now clear.

Chin throbbing, I inched my way towards the safe path, handhold by handhold. That the sun had warmed the rock, drying it out, was the only thing that made this possible – there was nothing resembling a level surface between me and the stairs. But at last I made it, and was able to climb, trembling, down to the Facility.

It was nearly featureless – an uninterrupted slab of gray cement, save for the few ventilation fans affixed to the roof and the reinforced steel door, painted olive drab, that greeted me as I approached the near wall. I was standing on a natural terrace of relatively flat rock, dotted with lichen and bird droppings. Water pooled in shallow depressions here and there despite the heat, but the terrace was otherwise devoid of interest – along with the gray wall and green door, it formed a bleak geometry that alienated the visitor more than any KEEP OUT sign could hope to do. Further discouragement was provided by the absence of a knob, latch or handle to open the door with. By all appearances, it was the kind of door intended exclusively for use as an exit – doubtless a crash bar was affixed to the other side.

Only the narrowest foothold separated the Facility's western wall from a sheer drop to the jagged rocks and churning sea below, so it was with great care that I edged around the side to check for an alternate entrance. There was none. The eastern side of the Facility was buried in the mountain, and I suspected the southern end was, too.

I gently touched my chin, and my fingers came away bloody. A pocket produced a wad of tissues, and I pressed these to the wound while I considered the mystery of this building. If the door I faced were the only entrance, and it could only be opened from the inside, then someone must be inside the building already – indeed, must be inside at all times. The only way for a visitor to get in would be for this person to know they were coming, and to leave the door open at a previously agreed-upon time. Perhaps the Facility was staffed in much the same way as the Station, with workers serving long stints there. Maybe more than one worker was on duty, so that they could take breaks. I could imagine one of them propping open the single door with a crate, and having a smoke out here on the terrace.

Imagining these workers inside monitoring various settings, examining data, striding around in their uniforms, gave me the idea that I should try simply knocking on the door. The Facility was large, but perhaps someone was stationed near this end – it was certainly reasonable to assume so.

I approached, arm extended, prepared to knock. But, before my knuckles could land, I heard a muffled buzz and click issue from beneath the painted steel, and the door fell silently open before me.

B eyond the doorway lay darkness. I took a step inside, instinctively feeling for a light switch or pull chain. None was evident. I reached around the door for the expected crash bar, and, reassured by its presence there, allowed the door to fall shut behind me with a dull thump.

The darkness was absolute now. I began to panic: I inhaled so sharply and hoarsely that I nearly choked, and sweat broke out under my arms. My scalp tingled with such intensity that I thought I could feel my hair turning brittle and gray.

What imagined horrors had frightened me, I didn't know – there was only terror, exerting itself on my body without first registering in my conscious thoughts. And then, as suddenly as it gripped me, the fear released me, leaving a fleeting feeling of euphoria in its wake. My muscles loosened and I let out a groan of relief.

As my mind grew accustomed to this temporary blindness, my other senses sharpened. The room I now stood in harbored a collection of familiar odors: engine oil, for one, specifically oil that had leaked for many years into a slab of wet cement. It was accompanied by the faint smell of gasoline, as though from a closed but poorly sealed five-gallon red plastic canister, with integral yellow spout. I could also detect rodents, possibly squirrels but probably mice, an active nest of them somewhere in the walls, and the mingled scents of insecticide and latex paint. Beneath it all lay a faint, fecal reek.

The quiet sound, of my boots scuffing against the cement, and of my once-panicked, now-calm breaths, echoed in a particular way against the floor and ceiling, giving me to reason that the space measured approximately twenty feet by fifteen, and that I was standing close to a wall. I reached out to my right, and my hand found a wooden shelf, cluttered with greasy, dusty cans and jars. I lifted one and gave it a shake, and heard the sound of small metal objects – nails, screws or washers – rattling inside glass. From somewhere nearby came the rhythmic thrum of a machine, though it didn't originate here, in this room – it came from behind a wall or walls. I also could sense something warm to my left, and remembered I'd heard a resonant tick when I entered, which had been repeating in ever-lengthening intervals. I set down the jar and reached out with my left hand. There it found a smooth metal surface, at about waist height: the hood, I realized, of a car. It was indeed slightly warm to the touch – as though the engine beneath it had been switched off about ten minutes before.

I didn't need light to know this was my father's 1982 Ford Mustang GT, but I slid my hand further across the hood to check for the scoop. There it was, as I expected – I could even feel the bumps along the edge where he'd touched up some chipped paint one summer afternoon, cursing as he did so at whatever or whoever it was that had caused the damage. In his lighter moments, my father used to explain to me, repetitively but fondly, how the scoop fed air to the engine, cooling it and making it more efficient, and how the spoiler on the back interfered with aerodynamic lift, keeping the rear tires more firmly in contact with the road, improving handling and performance. Many years later, I would repeat these lectures to a friend, who laughed, countering that such features were actually useless – just pretentious affectations designed to persuade insecure men that they possessed the skill and bravado of professional drivers.

Now that I understood where I was – the two-car garage of my childhood home in Hammond, Indiana – I didn't need the lights to guide me. I could navigate by memory alone. I stepped forward, dodging slightly to the left to avoid my sister's bicycle, which I knew was leaning against the wall beneath the shelves, felt my way towards the rear of Dad's car (he always backed in and expressed disdain for those who didn't), hopped up the two steps that separated the garage from the house, and threw open the door to the laundry room.

The washing machine and dryer were both running – obviously it was my mother's laundry day. A basket of clean clothes sat atop the dryer, ready to be folded, and I shuddered slightly at the sight of a pair of my father's white underpants, tangled up in a pair of faded jeans. I could detect the smell of a meal being cooked. Dinner would soon be served, and then my mother would tidy up while my father retreated alone to the living room to watch television. I would sit at the clean table, ammonia-scented patches of damp still evaporating from its surface, and do my homework while my mother folded the clothes.

At the end of the laundry room hung a painting of two people: a child, perhaps eight years old and of indeterminate gender, and a man. The man was tall and narrow-waisted and stood with his hand on the child's shoulder. Both figures gazed steadfastly at the viewer, with eyes that seemed slightly larger than normal. Each wore the tight-fitting checkered costume of a harlequin, in muted pastel colors, but only the man – the child's father, I always assumed – wore the character's familiar feathered cap.

Something about the child's bareheadedness always frightened me when I came in here to search for a favorite shirt from the dryer or basket – I imagined that the cap's absence was connected to some kind of drama. Perhaps the cap was a reward for some task the child hadn't completed, or it had been stolen. Or maybe the father had accosted the child while it was dressing or undressing. And their stances and expressions – at first glance, they appeared to be identically posed, but the longer I looked, the more I became convinced that the child appeared stooped, defeated, and had been, on some level, vanquished by the father's hand. And while the father's eyes conveyed a placid authority, the child's ostensibly identical gaze implied some fear or shame, or a silent plea for help.

I didn't like the painting. I'd asked my mother to remove it several times. But she said that it kept her company while she was doing laundry, and she left it there. Now that I was older, I didn't care so much about it, or perhaps I'd just learned not to look at it when I passed by, and that's what I did now: averted my eyes, opened the door, and entered the kitchen.

Mother was there, in her apron, standing at the stove, stirring something in a pot. She wore a dress – the kind she referred to as an 'everyday dress' but to me always seemed glamorous, perhaps to a fault. None of my friends' mothers wore dresses around the house all day. The fabric was slightly shiny and bore a floral print, and the pleats of the skirt waved gently back and forth as she stirred. Her hair, uncharacteristically, was let down, and brushed against her shoulders as she worked. Without turning around, she said, 'What have you been doing out there all this time?'

'What?'

Her shoulders fell, and she missed a cycle of stirring. Then, after a moment, she resumed.

'I thought you were your father. I heard the garage door.'

'He's here somewhere,' I said, opening the fridge and peering inside. 'His car's here anyway.'

'Don't eat anything. He wasn't in the garage?'

'The lights were off. What are we having?'

'Beef stew,' she said. She still hadn't turned around. I sat down at the table and let my backpack slide to the floor. 'Why are you so late?'

'I'm not that late. I had French Club.' This was a lie. I wasn't in French Club; I didn't know if there even was one. I'd been spending time alone after school walking in the woods, or going into town and ogling the guns and binoculars at the pawn shop, or trying to befriend the bums who maintained an encampment down along the train tracks where they crossed the canal. Once I realized I didn't have to account for my time in detail, I had stopped spending very much of it at home.

'This has been ready for twenty minutes,' my mother said, continuing to stir. 'Your sister went to Kelly's without telling me and now she's eating dinner there. You and your father just show up whenever. You want food to be ready when you want it to be ready, and if it isn't, you complain, and if it is, you just eat it and get up and leave again, and I don't know why I bother.'

'I'm sorry,' I said, though the behavior she was describing was almost exclusively my father's.

She fell silent. The food did smell good. I wanted to suggest that we just eat it together now, but neither of us wanted to find out what would happen if my father came in and found that we had started without him. Better to wait until he appeared, however late. His anger at having to eat reheated food was less severe, less persistent, than his anger at feeling left out or plotted against.

'French Club,' my mother said.

'Yeah.'

'Don't tell your father you're in French Club.'

'No.'

It was strange that my mother hadn't turned to look at me yet. Occasionally she would half hide her face if a friend of my sister's came over unexpectedly or if she had to sign for a package – 'I'm not together' is what she would say at these times, before letting her hair down and slightly mussing it with her hands, to conceal what I supposed she regarded as an inadequate amount of makeup, but which to me just looked normal. But no one else was in the house right now. I couldn't see anything of her neck above the collar, nor her cheek or nose or chin. I cleared my throat to try to get her to look at me, but she just kept stirring as we waited for my father to materialize.

I began to experience claustrophobia, of the sort one might feel if the walls had begun closing in, or some kind of white noise, a dark hiss, emanating from who knows where, had grown in volume until nothing else could be heard, though neither of these things were actually happening. The molecules that made up the air seemed to have grown larger, large enough so that each of them could be felt as it shuddered, spun, ricocheted around the room. I was finding it harder to breathe, and the monotony of my mother's stirring had begun to make me nauseous, as if I were on a boat inside the pot, floating upon the surface of the stew, bobbing and heaving with the rhythm of her stirring. My vision had begun to blur – but no, only my mother herself was blurring. The flowers of her dress flattened and ran together, as in one of the impressionist paintings we were supposed to memorize in art class, and her arm as it stirred smeared the air with its pigment.

'Mom?'

'I'm going to find him,' she spat, and she jerked the wooden spoon from the stew and flung it down onto the stove, dotting the countertop and backsplash with beef gravy. The spoon ricocheted off of the toaster and clattered to the floor. My mother turned abruptly, and her hair swung around to cover her face and stayed there as she passed. I could feel the giant particles of air parting to accommodate her as she flung open the laundry-room door and stomped through to the garage. The panic was returning now, beginning at the base of my spine, just outside the body, like an injection or parasite, and plunging in and up through my chest. I felt I might collapse, implode, as though I were tumbling to the bottom of the sea.

I knew what my mother would find. I realized now that I'd known it all along, that I'd seen but elected not to register the shape hanging from the rafters in the gloom of the empty half of the garage, and the faint glint of the kicked-over stepstool. 'Mom, wait,' I said, or thought I did; my mouth formed the words, but the breath had left me. Where had it gone? There: she had taken it. She was drawing it in, the way the sea pulls still water back and stands it up, suspends it before the crash. Her scream began as a percussive groan, as though she'd been punched; it stretched into a bass note, then gathered strength, rising in volume and pitch until it filled the house, my head, the world. That should have been me, out there, bearing witness. She didn't have to see it. And though it was too late, my body moved of its own volition, as though it thought it could turn back time. I stood up too fast, bashed my knee against the table leg, spun around and stumbled against the chair I'd just tipped over. The gray linoleum rose to meet me, and I could make out its many streaks and gouges, the dust and dead insects and bits of fallen food my mother didn't have time to clean. I closed my eyes, bracing for impact, but instead I passed through the floor and into darkness, as gravity, or something like it, pulled me from every direction.

Materiality reasserted itself slowly at first, then all at once, like a mountain emerging suddenly from fog. It took the form of rain on my face, a swale of green, a stone wall, and the calm gray sea; I was standing inside the shell of a ruined cottage on the island's western plain and gazing into the distant nothing. My body told me I had been here a long time, though my mind protested. I raised my trembling arm and studied my wristwatch. Two hours and forty minutes had passed since I entered the Facility on the rocky cliff, and I had missed my deadline again. ■

SECONDHAND

Mónica de la Torre

We take a limited number of routes, and only one of them could qualify as scenic. There is a dog park ten minutes away, and within a mile radius there are too many construction sites to keep track of. We live in a 'transitional neighborhood' in New York – Long Island City, the one Amazon snubbed after the local community demanded that its representatives stop kissing up to Jeff Bezos.

During one of our identical, unrepeatable walks, I began taking note of the miscellaneous oddities strewn about the pavement at the dog's eye level. It became a habit. Candy wrappers, cigarettes, alcohol nips, work gloves. Plastic bags, newspapers, discarded appliances, dog waste, sanitary gloves. In cold weather, the occasional winter glove, lost. Paired or solo, gloves kept appearing.

From then on, there has yet to be a day I haven't had multiple sightings of these stand-ins for the distracted train riders leaving them behind, the harried pedestrians dropping them, or the workers tossing them out when they are done for the day. These are people hired to service and build amenity laden condominiums in the gentrifying neighborhoods they themselves are being pushed out of, mainly in Brooklyn and Queens.

Eerily animated, it's as if the gloves persist in their attempt to express something that can't be reduced to words, something untranslatable. Let's call it absence, or avoidance of contact. For those who care to look down, and away from their devices, they act as an interface with the other side. ∎

nisex kids' gloves.

Puncture-resistant nitrile glove for goods packing.

Pair of multipurpose PVC-coated gloves, chemical-resistant.

Ultra-thin polyurethane-coated nylon safety glove for precision work.

Breathable polyurethane palm-coated work gloves with 360-degree cut protection.

Abrasion-resistant cotton-polyester glove with red smooth latex palm- and finger-coating for everyday jobs requiring basic protection.

Premium general-purpose glove with etched-rubber finish.

Disposable, non-sterile clear vinyl glove for wide-ranging janitorial and food services.

Slip-resistant SpiderGrip glove.

© TABITHA MOSES
Hairpurse, 2004
Photograph: Harriet Hall

HAIR

Mahreen Sohail

The boy's mother is sick and has lost all her hair. In solidarity, he decides to cut his off too. He thinks this is the least a son can do for a sick mother. The first person he tells is his girlfriend of one year. I'm going to donate my hair to my mother, he says, and is worried to see tears rise in her eyes. She had told him soon after they met that the first thing she liked about him was his shoulder-length hair, how it lay wild and free on top of his head, caused people on the street to glance back at them when they walked anywhere together. The boy worries that she is actually horrified at the idea of him cutting off his hair. *But it's my mother,* he thinks to himself, *it's my choice.* Before he can make a case the girl, a nice girl from a middle-class family who knows how to drop meaningful hints coyly (my parents are looking for a boy for me) finally says, I think cutting your hair for aunty would be a wonderful thing to do.

The mother is in bed with the smooth baldness of her newly shaved scalp, a scarf loosely draped across her neck. She does not know her son has gone to donate his hair, and is not the sort of mother who would approve if she did know. She does not believe one person being ill is the reason for another to act ill. And anyway, if she did know, she would have had enough faith in the girl to stop her son. She likes the girl. She thinks she is a good choice for her son, and maybe in a few years they will marry but the mother does not know if she will be alive for the wedding. A pure-cut line of steel runs through the mother and she knows the world moves on and on, so there is no need for theatrics, no need really for anything while she is so tired and in bed, staring up at the ceiling for hours on end, something she has only recently discovered is strangely meditative. Odd now to think that when her husband built the house she found the textured cream paint a little creepy, even said so to him then, The texture is a little creepy, a statement which the husband in his usual overbearing style, overrode. But now she understands why he chose the paint, maybe. It's easy for her to fall asleep while trying to follow the pattern it makes on the ceiling.

The salon is unisex. The boy and girl unclasp their hands when they enter and the boy explains at the counter what he wants. He says, I want to make sure my hair can be donated. His hair is tied up in the usual bun and he loosens it when he talks so the curls fall to his shoulders. I want it to be a wig for my mother. The woman behind the counter calls her associate's name and they descend on the boy and touch his head gently, with some sadness, as if he is their pet and they are about to say goodbye. Behind them, the girl stands with her own long, straight hair shining down her back, almost down to her knees. She rubs her arms as if she is cold, feels herself rising to the middle of this story and floating in the very center of it.

The husband watches the wife sleep. The house is nicest whenever she is asleep because he worries less about her and knows for a fact that she is resting, and for a little while at least he manages to forget that she is dying. This is more bearable than watching her lie awake and worry about dying. The husband is unsure if he has loved anyone in his life, at least in the way he thought he would love when he was younger, but now he thinks that maybe this is what love is supposed to be; you build a life around a person and when they threaten to go, you worry and worry that they will take you with them. If this is it, then he would prefer to go back to being a stranger to his wife.

The hairdresser winds his fingers through the boy's hair. He stretches out the curls, wets them with a spray bottle and combs through the hair with his fingers again. The boy looks at the man's face. Will it be possible? he asks. The man tries hard to look matter-of-fact, I'm sorry, he says, your hair has to be at least twelve inches long when the length is taken from the nape of your neck.

The girl feels her heart squeeze. The thing is – the thing is, she knows already that she wants to be with the boy, and while mostly her heart is compassionate for his family, some part of her is also thinking about how to make sure the boy will stay with her, *This is my time*, she thinks. The boy is nineteen years old this year, and like most nineteen-year-old boys seems not to know what he is doing and the girl is worried. She is eighteen, almost nineteen, and most of her friends are dating the men they believe they will marry. *Surely a man she is here for right now in the most impossible moment of his life will want her by his side forever*, the girl thinks. She rearranges her face so that it resembles a scissor, like something about to cut herself or the boy, and says, I'll do it. The boy looks at the girl's hair and says, You don't have to do this, but it is weak. They switch chairs and the hairdresser is swishing the towel around the girl's neck and spraying her hair with water and tying it in a ponytail at the nape of her neck.

Are you ready? he asks and she nods. Then he cuts it all off in two quick strokes. She closes her eyes for a second, but really she feels like a saint. She feels quite amazing, as if she has finally transcended petty relationships and is now in the midst of the truest, greatest love she is capable of.

The watching boy realizes he has made a big mistake. She looks terrible.

The wife does not open her eyes even though she feels she must get up soon to cook. She drifts in and out of consciousness during the day and the night, which the doctor had said was quite common at their last appointment, but even so it is easy to imagine that she will be better after this day passes. Maybe even in a few moments. I would love daal chawal, she says sleepily, actually wanting to get up and make it herself but her husband sitting by her side stands quickly. If you'll just go back to sleep, he pleads, I'll make it for you. He heads to the kitchen and pulls down the lentils from the top cupboard, pulls out the rice and looks at the two things for a moment. He wishes for a second that his son was home. It would be so lovely to have him here, both of them healthy and men, which sometimes feels like the natural order of things or if not the natural order of things at least some order of things.

The girl feels freer with the short hair. The hairdresser has not let the cut hair fall to the ground. He is still holding it in his fist so it descends like a black ribbon toward the floor. It can't touch the floor, he says, that's a no-no for wigs. We'll send it away and they'll mail you the wig in a week. The girl looks in the mirror at the boy's face and he seems ashen, absolutely wrecked, and again the girl feels triumphant. *This is it,* she thinks, *what a small sacrifice for him to fall in love with me!* The girl bargains in her head all the time about the boy – *if I do this he will do that, and if I do that he will do this* – so sometimes it can feel like he is lodged like a small, sharp rock in her head. The haircut has made his presence in her head lighter, as if a little bit of him has also been cut away with her hair.

The hairdresser puts the hair on a shelf, labels it with the boy's mother's name and he comes back to the girl. Her hair looks uneven. Would you like a bob-cut? he asks and she says, Sure. Riding on her high, she decides to try something fun. She gets an asymmetrical bob with the longer side touching her chin and the other side riding up to her ear. She does look a little experimental, like someone who could break up with the boy now, like she could live alone for a few years. The hairdresser asks if he can take a picture of her and she says, Yes, so he takes the towel off and swivels her around and uses a phone to take a picture. You'll find this online by this evening, he says and the girl beams. The girl and the boy hold hands out of the salon, their path lit up by the smiles of the salon staff.

Actually, the boy's hand feels like it is crawling with ants. These ants are coming out of his pores to protest. The girl looks horrible, he thinks, and he remembers how last night he had kissed her on her stomach and her back had arched a little off the bed and when it did her hair had lain thick under her, half on the mattress and half stuck to her spine, where he had brushed it off carelessly. The thing is the boy knows it is a terrible thing to like people based on their looks, and she is an amazing person. Which is worse, he wonders, to like someone less because they are ugly, or because they have become better than you during what is supposed to be the most character-building, mother-losing year of your life?

He decides while they drive home and as he takes sidelong glances at her, that he could like it more if it was a symmetrical bob. As if on cue she asks, Do you think it's too experimental?

The mother wakes and through a haze she can see her son and her husband and the girl standing there. The girl looks younger somehow. The husband is holding an entire plate of food and the smell of the food makes the mother sick. She turns on her side and vomits. I don't think your mother likes my hair, the girl says.

It looks great, the boy's father tells the girl, still holding the plate. Yes, the boy lies, it does. All three of them reach for the wastepaper basket filled with the vomit but none of them actually touch it. The mother pants, spent, on the bed.

That night the boy drives the girl back to her house. The maid opens the main door and avoids looking at the boy. The house staff is supposed to pretend the girl is pure and does not do anything with the boy except go out to public places and eat. The girl's parents pretend this too, or at least the mother does, and later she tells the girl's father, She will never get married if we keep her locked up in the house. Things have changed, and our daughter knows her limits.

The boy says hello to the girl's mother who is standing near the kitchen and the mother says hello back normally, but then her gaze falls on her daughter and she lets out a small scream, What did you do? The girl hesitates for a second, then speaks quickly, shyly, His mother needed a wig, and the mother, who is smart, understands why the daughter has done this, tries to redo her reaction so that she seems proud to have a daughter who can give this sort of sacrifice for the man she wants to be with, but really, the mother also feels immeasurably sad. All that long, beautiful hair.

The girl's hair is sent to a wig-maker in the middle of the city who threads each strand so it bands together again, coheres into a new shape for the recipient. The wig-maker reads the file of the recipient of the wig: 62; HOUSEWIFE. *Sixty-two-year-olds like layers in their hair,* he thinks so he cuts in a few layers and then gently puts the wig in crêpe paper, lays it down in a wooden box filled with small spheres of styrofoam. He tapes the box shut and presses on the address label.

The next day the boy kisses the girl on the lips when she is visiting his house. How's your mother? she asks when they are alone in his room and he says, Good, and then he kisses her again. When he puts his face near the side of the bob that is shorter, he feels as if something is missing, as if he is going out with a person without a limb.

I love this, he says and keeps kissing her, kisses her neck, easier to reach now, and she leans up and kisses him back. His parents are asleep in the other room so she bites his shoulder to keep from crying out during sex. Later when she sleeps, her shoulders and neck remain damp. He quietly gets out of bed and he takes scissors from his drawer. She is turned onto the side of her face with the shorter hair length. He lifts the longer hair from off her face and cuts it, taking care to hold the cut strands so they don't fall back on her face and wake her. The moment he cuts her hair he feels that deep satisfaction that only comes from having made something even again. She does look slightly better, though he's done a messy job. *This is fine,* he thinks, *it will grow back.* He throws the hair he has cut into the bin.

After throwing out the hair, the boy goes to his parents' room. The two of them are playing cards, though the mother has to be prompted to make a move by the father. Your turn, the father says every few minutes and the mother stares at him blankly before saying, Oh yes, and concentrating hard on the hand that she has been dealt. *Okay,* the boy thinks sitting on the bed with his parents, *They're fine.*

How is the girl? the father asks and the boy says, Good, good, good, three times in quick succession. He leaves to go back and watch the girl sleep.

Is this how sociopaths behave? He thinks about this while she is asleep and wonders if he could kill her if he had to and he thinks the answer is no, though you never know how you will react to things. This is the first girl he has ever slept with and he has cut her hair without permission. Who knows what else is inside him: a person who beats up women, a person who actually wants his mother to die now, a person who often wakes up thinking enough is enough.

The girl wakes and flies at him. She is ready to kill him: Are You Insane? and the father comes running: Why are you disturbing your moth— but he doesn't have time to finish his sentence because he is struck by his son's girlfriend's crying face and the fact that one side of her head looks as if someone has shorn a plant with little care. She looks like a small child who has been deliberately wounded. Suddenly, the father remembers again that he wanted to marry someone else when he was younger, a woman who lived nearby but his own mother at the time had said no, presenting instead this wife who he does love now and the father thinks that maybe this is what happens, we run circles around each other as a family, *young old young*, and here is his son in the middle of losing someone like he was once in the middle of losing someone and how they are both losing the mother *young old young*.

From the other room the mother calls and the girl leaves, still wailing. Without a word to each other the father and son present themselves to the dying woman and say, Everything is fine, You should go back to sleep.

The girl goes back home and falls into her mother's arms who says, What happened? but not before running her hand over the girl's head. This is the thing, the mother says, you gave him too much power, and the girl says, What power? And the mother who knows that the daughter will have to cobble together a dynamite personality one day to get through life successfully – remember if Mohammed cannot go to the mountain the mountain will come to Mohammed, the winner is always a man named Mohammed – but her poor baby, My poor baby, she says. She cradles her daughter's head in her lap and says softly, It will grow back, as if hearts are things that grow back and men are roots you can pull out of the ground and toss away.

The wig arrives at the house on a day when the father and the son are home and the mother is feeling better. The father brings in the box and puts it on the bed and carefully cuts the tape on the carton with a little razor blade, sets that aside and opens the box, pushes aside the crêpe paper. He moves the box onto the mother's lap. With a cry of delight the mother lifts up the wig with her bruised hands. It's beautiful, she says patting the hair, Oh, it really is beautiful. She begins to cry and tells the boy, You must call her and tell her she is beautiful. She takes off her scarf and fixes the wig on her head and by the doorway, her son leans against the door. For a second the only thing the room consists of is how happy his mother is.

When they bury her, they bury her with the wig. The girl does not come to the funeral, having transcended the relationship enough by then to be telling her friends I was dating a psychopath.

The boy even calls the girl and tells her about the funeral before it happens, but she hmms and haws having discovered some hardness in the story, some new asphalt to coast on. She is learning that she does not want to settle into adulthood with nothing to show for her youth except some pictures of herself in varying poses with hair at different lengths. Here it is long, here it is short, here it is gone and now it's back again. She is learning not to be kind for the sake of being kind and her mother is sad about this hardness that has arisen in her daughter, but you cannot unlearn a lesson, and her daughter is already practicing how to wield this lesson in the world.

The boy breathes a sigh of relief immediately after the funeral and wonders about all the paths to tragedy. For example, the hair was dead when it became a wig and for a while, in-between, when she got better for a week, his mother used to hang it up on the coatrack carefully at night and he would imagine that because it was dead hair, it would soon begin to fall, strand by strand onto the floor.

By now, the boy thinks after a month has passed, *it must be caked in mud so many feet deep in the ground, damp and splitting.* Or maybe if he and his father dug up the grave in a year's time there would be nothing there at all except the hair once given from a woman to a woman, still long, shining and straight, also some bones.

The girl's hair grows. She oils it with coconut oil nightly, sometimes uses yogurt and fenugreek. It grows down her back, and for her wedding three years later she has it up in a princess braid, pinned a thousand different ways so her husband has to spend the first two hours of their wedding night helping her take it out. It crackles hard with hairspray underneath her when they lie in bed together, too tired to touch. When they divorce three years later, she cuts it off, so it looks like a boy's, dyes it bright red so people say, This is what happens, in whispers behind her back. She travels soon after, the dye fading now in the short stumpy hair, feeling invisible and light.

The hair is just touching her shoulders when she meets someone again. It grows faster than it has ever grown when she is in love and happy, when she is pregnant with her first daughter.

The girl and her husband shave their daughter's head four days after the birth. Her husband holds the baby's head as if it is a bird, the blade sharp and keen across the soft malleable temple.

When the girl breastfeeds her daughter, her hair begins to turn white, as if the baby is leeching the color out, and soon it is falling in thick clumps and sticking to the shower drain. Pregnancy hair is short-lived, a friend – a mother three times over by then – tells her on the phone. The girl cuts it off again. Then it grows slowly. She lets it wisp onwards for years, through new jobs, illnesses, nights spent lying awake, her mother's death, and then begins to dye it black. She asks her daughter if she looks like Madonna, *young old young*, and the daughter (now a teen) says, Who is Madonna?

When the girl dies, it is this daughter who bathes her, who curls shampoo into the soft wrinkles set deep in her mother's still scalp. Hope is always a daughter with an unbroken heart. In the distance the line of mountains snakes on across the horizon and reaches singing for the women too. ■

Lookingoutof, 2018
UNION Gallery

LEARNING TO SING

Lydia Davis

You are in a neighborhood singing group, you are singing with the others for recreation, for pleasure, not in order to perform. You enjoy it, but you are not satisfied with the way you sing. You would like to learn, at least, better control of your legato, your dynamics, your phrasing, and maybe, if you can, how to produce a better quality in your voice itself. You can read music quite easily, and you do sing on pitch, but your voice is thin and weak. One of the group suggests, after a while, that you might want to find a good singing teacher. She has a name for you.

You think it will be simple to learn to sing better. You will go to this good teacher, take lessons and practice. She is in the next town to the north, the wife of a minister. She is very experienced and was once the coach, down in the city, to singers of opera. The lessons will take place in a room in the parsonage. You think that over time you can't help, then, but learn to sing better.

But it is not so simple. You discover during your very first lessons that the problem of singing better involves overcoming many other problems you had not ever imagined: the problem of your breathing, of how you stand, how you hold your body, how you hold your neck.

You try blowing on a candle. This is to teach you to control your breath. She has you blow steadily on the flame of a candle to see if you can make it flicker evenly. The weather is too hot to do this, it is the middle of summer, and it is, or feels like, the hottest summer you have ever experienced. But you do it. She has you expel all your breath before you inhale and sing. You should inhale as though you were sucking in the air through a straw. She asks you to watch yourself inhale in the mirror while holding your shoulders with your hands.

You are tense. You are so tense with yourself! she says. She asks you to turn your knees out and bounce, and to keep your knees slightly bent and flexible. Then she brings out a small trampoline and has you jump on it. She has you sing as you jump up and down. This is supposed to loosen you up. She says, Yes, yes! She lends you the trampoline, you take it home, and jump up and down on it in the living room as you sing your scales.

You sing scales and practice the song that she has assigned you, an aria by Handel. It is a famous one, though you had not known it before. It is a beautiful aria that begins with the open syllable *La–*, and the first notes are comfortably within your range. You are moved by it. But when you sing it, the sounds you make are not pleasing. There on the page, as you read them, are notes that form a beautiful piece, but it is beyond your ability to create that beauty. It is your voice that is in the way. Your voice skips like the needle on a record. It squawks on some of the high notes. It is like something broken. She asks you to imagine that your voice, as it sings the melody, is a continuous golden thread.

Your teacher lends you a book on how to relax. But you are too impatient to try the exercises. You like to be active, and learning to relax is not active enough. Day after day you do not try them. You are aware of the book lying there in plain sight. Then you try one, and it seems to work. You make a good plan: you will do one exercise each day before you practice your singing. Now you begin to dread practicing and you begin to avoid it. So you drop the relaxation exercises. Some days you are pleased, when singing at least a few notes, by the sound of your voice. On other days you are very distressed, feel your heart sink and want to cry. The unpleasant sounds are so audible, so loud, so public, even in your own living room, in private, in your own ears.

Your teacher recommends that you try the Alexander technique. You make an appointment to see the teacher of the Alexander technique, but she is very late for the appointment, too late for the lesson. You go again to see her. She discusses with you the problem of your tension, how tense you are in your life, but, more importantly, the problem of how you regard other people and how you regard yourself. You are so tense with yourself! says the teacher of the Alexander technique. You are so tense with yourself! says the singing teacher again.

And why are you so critical? asks the singing teacher. Who was critical of you in your life? You think about it, but not for long. Of course, you know it was your mother. But it was your father, too – he did not disagree with your mother. It was also, sometimes, your older sister – though not your brother.

Your teacher assigns you a song by Schubert. You know his songs very well, and many of them you like – they are satisfying in their harmonies and structures, though not moving to you. But you are holding your breath before you sing, and you shouldn't. You are taking a breath, a shallow breath, and holding it, and then singing. You should expel all the air first, take a deep breath and immediately sing, as if immediately rolling down the other side of a hill. You are trying too hard, your teacher says. Who made you try so hard, in your life? You are assigned a song by Stefano Donaudy and then another song, one by Fauré you have never heard before. In fact, you did not know the songs of Fauré, only the *Requiem*, and they become a new love. They are more moving to you than the songs by Schubert. You listen to them over and over again, as sung by Véronique Gens.

Your throat is dry, so the teacher has you take a drink of water. You take sips of water, then you burp in the middle of a scale. You can't practice without sipping water, but you can't sip water without burping. Your teacher suggests that you drink more clear fluids throughout the day and eat fresh horseradish.

Then she suggests that you see a doctor to check your nose and throat, to make sure nothing is wrong with your throat, because sometimes your voice skips.

You make an appointment. You sing more songs by Fauré. You have not forgotten to think about your tension and why you are tense. But you have one small worry: if you cease to be tense, perhaps you can't go on doing the other things in your life the way you have always done them. Do you really want to change? Do you want to relax enough to be able to sing better, but lose the tension you need to do everything else? But perhaps that won't happen.

You hope the ear, nose and throat specialist will find something wrong, but not very wrong. It should be something simple enough for you to correct it, so that then the quality of your voice will improve.

You sit in the specialist's office with a small camera up your nostril. A young resident watches your larynx and asks you to sing a note and then a higher note. The doctor who is training the young resident sings along with you. The voice problem turns out to be, possibly, not a voice problem but a stomach problem and you are given some pills to take, one each morning. You take one the next morning. Then, when you read more about the possible complications of continuing to take them, you put them away and never take another one.

The weeks are passing and you are practicing quite regularly. You practice in the living room, standing up, always when you are alone. If someone comes into the house, by chance, they are startled by your voice, so loud in the small house, and you stop. You may be improving, very slightly. What this actually means is that most of the time, you are singing in just the same way as always, your voice thin and weak, even tremulous, but that every now and then a few notes are round and full, though not yet rich.

Your teacher tells you that you must learn to sing from your chest, specifically from your breastbone. She tells you about what she calls *appoggia*, which, she says, means leaning into the sound.

She tells you to sing sitting down, to sit back on your spine. She has you sing sitting down, with the weight of your torso on your distal

– though you don't know what that means. When the singing is better, she asks you, What did you *do*? But even when you like the sound you are making, it is thin, which to you means young.

You think what is involved is also to sing more like a woman. Maybe you have been singing like a young girl. Maybe you are in fact more like a girl than a woman. You don't know exactly what you think you are. It could also be that you think you're a boy, but it is almost certainly not that you think you're a woman. It is hard for you not to feel like a young girl, anyway, standing in front of this teacher, who is larger than you and also seems older because she is a teacher, even though in fact she is younger, though only by a few months. In the first lessons, she kept saying how small you were, though you would never describe yourself as small. You are almost sure, though you don't want to ask her, that singing better also involves being more womanly, or more like a woman. You wonder if it would help to be larger. Or at least to think of yourself as larger.

The teacher of the Alexander technique, when you see her one more time, tells you to put two pillows under your T-shirt, one in front and one in the back, and practice your singing that way. The singing teacher points to a buxom statue on her piano, in order to give you the idea. It is too hot to do that, you think, it is the middle of summer, and the hottest summer in many years. You do it anyway, but there is no change in the way you sing. You remark on this to your teacher. Your teacher laughs, because you expect everything to happen right away.

She asks, another time, if you are patient. Within certain limits, you can be.

You are trying to learn to stand up straight and keep your chin down, as she has instructed. You tell her this. But not too far down, she answers. On the other hand, you keep forgetting to let your voice 'drop' into your chest, into the area of your breastbone – that is, you keep forgetting about the *appoggia*, which means 'leaning in'.

How does she have the wisdom, you wonder, not to comment until now that you should not be singing the triplets, three against two, quite so deliberately, so correctly? You don't understand how to fix that. Then, you think you see what she means, when you listen more carefully to Véronique Gens singing the first Fauré song. You wish, yet again, that your voice were good enough so that you could concentrate, with your teacher, on musical interpretation rather than on simply producing an acceptable sound.

Then, after some months of this, on through the winter and into the spring, it is time to prepare for a recital. You are not the only one who has been studying with your singing teacher. Most of her pupils are high school students – there is only one other older woman. Some of them sing well, especially one tenor with a truly beautiful voice. Listening to him sing, you understand what it means to be moved almost to tears just by the quality of a voice. All her pupils will take part in a recital. You are willing – you know it is a good thing to work toward a performance. Now there is more practicing and then there is rehearsing.

In the recital, you are to play the part of a lady attendant on the Queen of the Night, one of three attendants. That is all right with you. You like singing in harmony, which was why you joined the neighborhood singing group in the first place. Each pupil, however, is also to sing a solo and your teacher has asked you to sing the Handel aria that you learned in your first lessons. You agree to do it, because you think that this, too, must be a good thing for your musical practice, and also for your character, but you are nervous. She teaches you the small ornaments you should add when phrases are repeated, and she works out certain expressive hand gestures for you to use, though these seem to you rather artificial.

In addition to singing it from memory, there is another challenge. It has one rather high note that you must land on after a leap of a large interval. There is no way to make sure that you will land on it successfully, without squawking. About half the time, practicing at home alone, you don't squawk when you sing it, and half the time you do. You can guess that you will be tenser than usual onstage, in the church, in front of the assembled audience, even though they will be mostly families and friends of the young performers. You will be alone there, except for your teacher accompanying you at the piano nearby. You will be alone with a fifty-fifty chance of emitting an embarrassing squawk. Still, you are willing to try.

The recital takes place, and as it goes along, each pupil does well. The teacher has prepared them carefully. After the piece in which you play the part of the lady attendant, you change out of your costume and into your formal clothes and stand in the wings waiting for your turn to sing the aria. You are certainly nervous, but you expected that. Then you walk out, and you sing the aria. You don't forget any of it, though you come close. You remember the hand gestures and the ornaments. When the moment comes for you to land on the high note, you do land on it without squawking, though not with a lovely sound, and you finish singing the aria, to your great relief. After the polite applause dies down, your teacher unexpectedly addresses the audience and lets them know that you began your lessons only the previous summer and have never before sung a solo onstage in public. She is proud of you, you know. The audience applauds politely again.

After the recital, there will be a break in your lessons, since summer has come again, the high school students are away, working at their summer jobs, and you, as well as the teacher, need to rest for a little while from the intensity of the practicing and the rehearsals. Several weeks later, you return to the parsonage, but now you are preparing to move away from the area, and when you do, that will be a natural end to your singing lessons. You are left with the knowledge that improving your singing ability would not be a simple matter, if you tried it again. You no longer have the illusion that by taking lessons and working diligently you could steadily improve your singing. Still, you may try again.

As for the recital, when you think back on it you still experience the same dread and nervousness, since there was never any guarantee that you would land gracefully on that note. It is true that you worked hard on the piece, and you did all you could, out there on the stage, to sing every note of the aria as you had been taught, but there was always an element of chance about your singing it successfully. You might just as well have made a dreadful squawk as you landed on the high note. That note would have been completely isolated in space, and in the attention of everyone listening, as isolated as any sound you had ever made, and it would have echoed through the vast spaces of the church, to your great embarrassment. That is why you continue to hear it in your imagination, and suffer it, though the recital is by now safely in the past. ∎

COLLECTIVE

While you're away the rules will change. Overnight the town
becomes a fortress, your marriage a morgue. Spies are installed
in adobe walls and a new tax is levied on sleep. Your daughters
are taken from their beds and you stand for hours to offer bills
of surrender. Down the hall a mason builds a chamber to incubate
memories. The treasury starts trading currency for cigarettes
and a light bulb keeps track of infidelities. Your body –
that mountain you carry around, begins to develop craters.
One day your heart will collapse, this economy too, but for now
a man in a pink ballgown is restoring lost matchsticks to their boxes.
When the final bell rings and the curtains part, we climb a ladder
together. Some stand above to measure the wind. Makers of bread
take subsidiary rungs. No doubt we'll change positions. A king
may drink from a beggar's well, the sweeper's wife will emerge
from the leeward side in a three-piece suit and tie. Try not to search
for meaning. If you need proof you're alive, regard the oar
in your hand. Look at all this glass, the vaulted ceiling.
Someone is hammering a skylight in the roof.

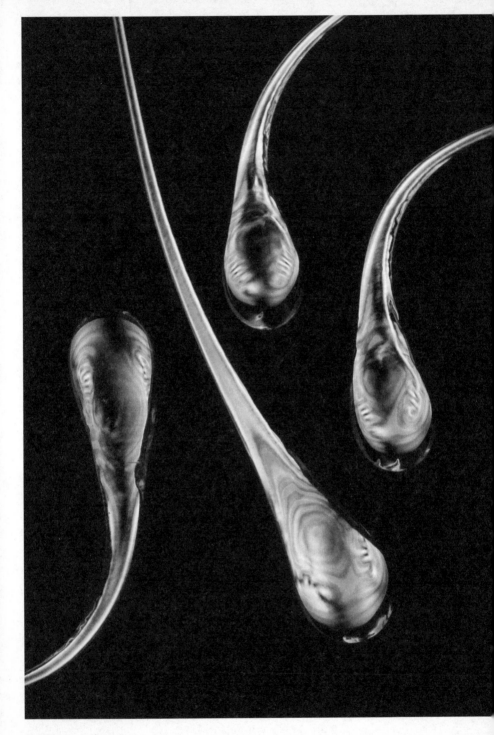

SNAP

Anouchka Grose

1

I still don't understand why I minded so much that Harvey had fucked another woman. It was right at the beginning, before he gave me my own toothbrush at his flat. We had no agreement about what we were doing with each other. Still, when I found out about it three years later, I felt pulverised. No matter how hard I tried, I couldn't unbreak what was broken – perhaps because I found it so hard to grasp quite what it was.

2

In his 1921 essay 'Group Psychology and the Analysis of the Ego', Freud makes fleeting reference to a 'Prince Rupert's drop'. Describing the sudden, panicked dissolution of an army at the moment when the leader is lost, he writes: 'The group vanishes in dust, like a Prince Rupert's drop when its tail is broken off.'

Also known as 'Batavian tears', these little tadpole-shaped glass droplets have puzzled physicists for centuries. The bulbous end is strong enough to withstand being shot or repeatedly beaten with a hammer, but if you snip off the spindly tail – which can be accomplished with an ordinary pair of scissors – the whole thing explodes into powder. How could an object simultaneously be so indestructible and so fragile?

Made in north Germany by dripping molten soda lime or flint glass into water, the drops were first brought to Britain in 1660 by Prince Rupert of the Rhine, who gave five of them to King Charles II. He passed them on to the Royal Society, where Constantijn Huygens asked the author/scientist/philosopher/poet/fancy-dresser Margaret Cavendish to establish what was going on with the curious glass beads. She concluded, wrongly, that they must contain a core of volatile liquid that vanished on contact with air.

In 2016, the mystery was finally solved using integrated photoelasticity, which illuminated the stress lines inside the droplet in glowing rainbow bands, allowing scientists to track 'the repeated bifurcation' of 'self-propagating cracks' that lead to the shattering. Armed with this new information they finally understood what had been holding the droplets together in such a peculiar way. Everything is set in place at the first moment of contact with water: the surface of the molten glass cools and contracts faster than the core, creating an outer layer that presses inwards. This is counterbalanced by the centrifugal push of the slower-to-cool heart. This results in a very particular distribution of stresses, beginning with the highly compressive tensions on the rounded surface of the drop which leave the warmer, still agitated molecules too little space. These are then compacted into one another, creating an incredible suspended energy at the nucleus of the drop. An alteration to the overall balance of forces releases them from their perfect state, but this can only be effected from a particular point – the spindly tail – below which the unlikely and uncomfortable interrelation of molecules proves stubbornly unshakeable.

Without any knowledge of the dynamics at work in the droplet, Freud nonetheless managed to employ the metaphor perfectly. It's an example of his astonishing, infuriating capacity to extrapolate the imperceptible from the perceptible without being able scientifically to prove the link. He explains that there are invisible forces at work holding groups of people together, but that these are inevitably offset by forces that split them apart. In a large, organised group like an army, people might appear to be held in perfect formation by their multidirectional allegiances to one another and to their leader, but this can change in an instant. If, in order to function together, they have put aside their greed, rivalry and rapaciousness for the sake of the greater good, these disavowed characteristics might suddenly reappear due to a shift in conditions. The example Freud uses is the immediate dispersal of the Assyrian army on hearing that general Holofernes has lost his head: 'The loss of the leader . . . brings on the outbreak of panic . . . the mutual ties between the members of the group disappear, as a rule, at the same time as the tie with their leader.' Without their commander around to give orders, enforce rules and bolster the idea of a higher purpose, the individual soldiers are no longer compelled to be ultra-disciplined, and may revert to being regular, self-interested individuals. Whereas the army might have sustained itself with the notion of its members being extraordinarily good to one another while being extraordinarily bad to their adversaries, now the ex-members could choose to be good or bad to anyone according to their own drives and impulses. They might steal from, or trample over, their compatriots in an instantaneous outbreak of egoistic voracity. Equally, they might become terrified that former friends would suddenly turn on them.

As Freud had stated six years earlier, 'Hate . . . is older than love.' He argues that the human organism is originally repelled by anything that comes at it from the outside – anything that isn't itself – but gradually learns to tolerate, even to love, the encroachments the world inflicts on it. Still, the underlying revulsion never fully goes away, but is simply held in check, ready to be activated by circumstance; we're all soldiers, drilled to walk in formation but ready to break ranks, smash and destroy, if ever we spot the right opportunity.

Three pages on in the 'Group Psychology' essay, where Freud begins to dismantle all the ideas he has only just proposed (such as the structural importance of a leader to a group), he refers to Schopenhauer's famous freezing porcupines, drawn together by their need for heat, but pushed apart by their prickles until, according to Schopenhauer, 'they had discovered a mean distance at which they could most tolerably exist'. Here, Freud claims, 'The evidence of psychoanalysis shows us that almost every intimate emotional relation between two people which lasts for some time – marriage, friendship, the relations between parents and children – contains a sediment of feelings of aversion and hostility, which only escapes perception as a result of repression.' For Freud, it is fundamentally impossible for people to love one another unambiguously. Aggression, hatred, repulsion, rivalry *always* coexist alongside – or underlie – attachment, cooperation and affection. The closest, most life-sustaining bond is haunted by its opposite; a helpless newborn, desperately needing sustenance and protection, is also bound to be aggravated by touch, sickened by suckling, enraged by the frustrating action and inaction of its carers.

Babies scream because life hurts, attachments disappoint, the world is one gigantic, up-in-your-face horror. This is what you notice first, before socialisation attempts to persuade you otherwise. And then, if all goes well, you forget. Things become organised, start to make sense, appear tolerable, controllable even. You come to like, love, trust, lean on the people who have inflicted this weird existence on you. Or at least you are prepared to overlook a great deal of difficulty in order to sustain your alliances.

Love is never unequivocal. So it stands to reason that a part of me must have disliked Harvey all along. I'd just been waiting for the right conditions to unleash my hatred on him. But what made these particular conditions *so* right?

3

It's New Year's Eve 1976, five days before my seventh birthday. My family are at the same event we go to every year: a party at my godmother's place in Gloucestershire. She has by far the biggest house of anyone we know: an ersatz stately home – a Victorian copy of a Georgian pile – complete with columns, gamekeeper's lodge, lake, folly, even a ha-ha. She has always seemed to me a supremely calm, kind, blow-dried woman. My sister and I have been told that this is the family we would live with if both our parents died. It's a spectacular house, but we very much hope our mum and dad will stick around to bring us up. We've read *Cinderella, Hansel and Gretel, Snow White*, and are fully indoctrinated into the belief that biological parents are best. You wouldn't want to be left in the clutches of someone who was probably only pretending to care about you as a favour to someone else, however serene and elegantly coiffed they might appear.

It's the early part of the evening, when children are still allowed in the drawing room. We've never stayed up till midnight – not at New Year's Eve or any other time. It's all a bit of a mystery what goes on then, but the signs are a little worrying. My mum, dad and I are sitting around the end of a long, mahogany dining table, with me at the head. Kate Dartford – Levi's mum – is perched on my dad's lap, directly across from my mum. The reason for this, ostensibly, is that there aren't enough chairs to go round. I would be very happy to move, to sit on my mum's lap and give Levi's mum the chair, but it all becomes a big, awkward joke about space and chairs and laps. I have the idea that my mum is deeply uncomfortable, although it might just be me. I also think Levi's mum is acting a little weirdly. Is she laughing too much to cover something up? Does she want to stay there? Or is she biding her time till she finds a way to excuse herself? I feel frightened and angry. It's hard to see what's making us all agree to this. Why would my dad take the risk? By showing my mum and me what it might look like if all the relations between us suddenly changed – if Levi's mum was the correct person for him to have on his lap, and my mum and I were separate from him and from each other – it's as if he's issuing a threat. The question is whether he knows he's doing it, or whether his enjoyment is blinding him to the possible significance of the seating arrangement. In either case I hate him for it. It doesn't take much to snap the tail and, before you know it, everything's broken.

At ten o'clock, it's time for the children to disappear. This particular house has about fifteen bedrooms, some of which are spooky and only semi-furnished, while others are flamboyantly decorated and welcoming. The children are guided towards the shabby rooms at the top of the house, the lower-down ones being reserved for more esteemed visitors. We're quite used to this – we know that *they* eat better food, wear better clothes and sleep in better rooms than us. My sister and I always wake up early after parties in our own house to steal the chocolates, Bath Oliver biscuits and real butter that would otherwise never make an appearance in our lives.

As soon as we feel we've left enough time to make the adults believe we're sleeping, we reconvene in one of the best bedrooms and look for ways to amuse ourselves. This particular bedroom has a number of spectacular features: an en-suite bathroom with bidet, Liberty peacock-patterned wallpaper, a plume of real peacock feathers (collected from the peacocks in the garden), low lighting, a huge bed and a chintzy antique china washing bowl and jug.

I have no idea how we came up with that night's special activity. I don't think there was a leader telling us what to do. There were probably a few abortive attempts at fun – wink murder, bouncing on the bed – before it all came about quite haphazardly, one idea building on another until we hit upon the perfect enterprise. An en-suite bathroom obviously had potential – there were bottles, taps, Crabtree & Evelyn soaps and lotions. The game involved gathering tissues, cotton wool and loo paper, soaking them in either the jug or the bowl and throwing them at the wall. You could cram a lot of violence into the launch – you wanted your missile to land with a satisfying splat – but then the slow creep down the wallpaper was unexpectedly mesmerising. It turned out to be the game that had everything. You could play it competitively or non-competitively, either going up against one another on the grounds of bundle size and hit height, or noodling away in a corner, perhaps making 3D polka dots or spirals. It was all at once a physics experiment, a protest, an art form and an act of catharsis.

I suppose we must have become a bit noisy. Or maybe it was the light under the door. Or perhaps we just kept going till after midnight when someone came up to collect us. Anyhow, eventually we were discovered. My godmother screamed and ranted, unleashing on us what seemed to me a pure form of hate. Naturally, she was angry at her own children, but they would never have done it without us. We were foul, destructive, despicable, thoughtless. Couldn't we see the blisters forming in the new wallpaper? The murky stains along the edge of the pale carpet? Why, why, why? What was *wrong* with us?

Thank goodness my parents were, are, still alive and we were never thrown to the mercy of this woman. Having seen the flip side of her immaculate exterior, I suspected she might not have had the wherewithal to love us in quite the right way.

My mum and dad also stayed together, confounding my almost constant suspicion: why did my dad sometimes join us late on holiday, apparently due to some unforeseeable last-minute work emergency? Did he *really* have to crash-land his glider and wait in a field to be rescued, having phoned home from a call box, *every* other Sunday? What kind of conversation was my mother having with my godfather, so close together on the garden wall that sunny afternoon? There were secrets, I was sure, but accessing them seemed impossible. You couldn't ask outright, and everything clung together too well for the underlying forces ever to be exposed.

4

Since looking up Batavian tears I've occasionally found myself wondering about the original gift to the king. It *can't* have been just five drops, although this is what history tells us. If Charles II gave five to the Royal Society then surely there must have been at least six. Wouldn't you need to shatter one for the gift to be credible? Maybe there were ten . . . fifteen . . . a hundred. Perhaps Rupert and Charles sat around cracking them all afternoon before they decided to preserve the last handful. And how many did the scientists then have to smash before they felt satisfied with their fantastical, speculative theories? Did they enjoy destroying the delicate, pretty little trinkets belonging to the king? What a strange, terrible, exciting present – something you have to defile in order to appreciate.

5

It's almost impossible to paraphrase Freud without feeling like you're missing out all the important bits. Every part seems to depend on every other part – and this is in spite of what Freud himself called his 'Viennese *Schlamperei*', referring to a kind of slapdashness born from trying to jot too many ideas down too quickly. (Pressurised, like hot glass in cold water?)

Having made his point about the formational importance of the leader to the group, and the multiple nature of the ties that bound the members to one another, Freud was confronted by the question of the nature of the ties themselves. Were they instinctive or learned? What were they made out of? He proposed a number of possibilities. They might be straightforwardly libidinal/erotic ties – you may have the idea that you could get some form of sensual satisfaction from the members of your group, hence your wish to keep them around. Alternatively, they might be 'aim-inhibited erotic ties', where the voluptuous aspect of the pull towards the other person has been repressed, leaving you freer to coexist in a calm state. Then again, there's the possibility of an identificatory tie – the others are somehow 'like you'. But would this necessarily make you want to hang out with them? (All these ties date from a post-infantile developmental phase, once one's basic temperament has morphed from indiscriminate hate to more nuanced likes and dislikes . . .)

Freud attempted to untangle all this using the format of the conventional family, which seems a reasonable enough idea given that it's where most humans are built. So, to set out with the quintessential, biologically underpinned, heterosexual economic unit, we begin with a boy who is sensually attached to his mother. At around three years old, as his drives and sense of self develop, this attachment becomes particularly intense – perhaps because he now understands some of the threats to it: other siblings, his father, the fact that his mother could abandon him or die. Without exactly knowing it, he begins to strategise; it's probably better to be nice to your siblings, that way your mother and father will like you more. You develop what Freud calls 'reaction formations' – the more you hate something, the more you may decide to force yourself to love it. Eventually this performance will become so convincing that even you believe in it, completely forgetting the antipathy that underpins your solicitousness. This operation relies on an observer – a 'leader' – who makes it worth your while. This 'leader' may be your mother, your father, or both. But why should you want to please your father? Aren't you supposed to be trying to kill him?

Of course it's not so simple. You might try to get your father out of the way, perhaps by having nightmares so that your mother will sleep in your room. Still, this is unlikely to give you exactly what you want – especially because your child mind isn't at all precise about what that is. Another cunning way to deal with the father problem would be to be a bit more like him – that way your mother might like you in the way she seems to like him (if indeed she does). At the same time as recommending yourself to your mother, you also demonstrate to your father that you think he's got something worth copying. Now both parents are on side. But identification is brilliantly double-edged. As the American academic Diana Fuss puts it: 'At the base of every identification lies a murderous wish: the subject's desire to cannibalize the other who inhabits the place it longs to occupy.' This wish is obscured by the implicit compliment: You're so great, I want to be just like you.

So to return to the original question of the kinds of joins that operate between the individual members of a group (even a group as small as a family or, to compress down to the smallest possible unit, the couple that predates the family) Freud gives us an array of options, plus the idea that some of the options will overlap and elide. You have the possibility of a straightforward libidinal tie, typified by a child's sensual attachment to its mother, but which can also find itself aimed at a sibling or father. In turn, this tie will be disavowed – children are told off for this sort of thing – and replaced by the more serviceable 'aim-inhibited' version. Then again there's the sort of bond that grows out of its opposite – a guilefully 'caring', 'empathic' reaction formation. And finally an ambiguous, ambivalent identificatory tie, simultaneously deadly and admiring.

The conflicting attractions, repulsions, disavowals and demonstrations are consciously experienced as something much simpler and more cohesive. It would be far too difficult and upsetting to look below the surface and see what your attachments are actually made out of. Much better to accept things at face value and uncritically 'love' your family, your school friends, your home town, your partner, your job, your religion, your country. Once you start to question these things it all just becomes too confusing and painful.

Having said that, it's not as though you can fool yourself forever. Something inevitably punctures the veneer. You feel frustrated, bothered by all the things you've pushed to one side. Perhaps you become so exhausted from maintaining the inside of your group, or family, or couple, that you start to look for something outside it. Or you get together to destroy another group to help yourselves feel internally fortified. Or you introduce something annoying from the outside to remind yourself why the inside is preferable. Or someone else brings in something from the outside and all the internal defences you've built to hold the group together are suddenly dismantled; you re-encounter the repressed, forgotten, disavowed primacy of hate.

6

Insofar as I could tell, before the new information, I simply and straightforwardly loved Harvey. In fact, I would have said I loved him thoroughly, absolutely, totally. And this was in spite of a good working knowledge of psychoanalysis. As Freud also teaches us, our passion for ignorance is boundless; any knowledge we gain is liable to be trounced by wishful thinking.

Harvey had an other-worldly naivety that made me trust him without question. Because of his work we were often apart, but I never worried about what he got up to. Whenever he was there he felt really *there*, and that was enough for me. So when one day he said, 'I kind of started going out with someone around the same time I started going out with you, but it was only for a few weeks,' I almost lost my mind. I stormed around his flat. I swore at him. I punched his sofa. I don't think he understood my reaction. But then again, neither did I. She was hardly a threat to the relationship in any real sense; it was already a thing of the past. The issue was more that I found the whole idea intensely repulsive. I immediately referred to the woman as 'scuzzy' without knowing a single thing about her. It's actually more likely – given Harvey's tastes and foibles – that she was perfectly well-laundered and pleasant, but to me in that moment the very idea of her stank. She probably carried diseases. Hadn't I had repeated bouts of thrush in those first weeks?

There was one thing I knew for sure, she wasn't *one of us*. She had infiltrated our precious, border-controlled, two-person society. (And what is a couple if not the most perfect, compact group – the minimum quantity of people required to begin to organise, to police, to gang up, to feel that there's safety in numbers? But who was the leader, Harvey or me? Each of us seemed to think it was the other, and put a great deal of underhand effort into redressing the perceived imbalance.) I despised this alien with my entire being.

'But it wasn't really a thing,' said Harvey. 'It was just a mistake on my part. I didn't know I was going to fall in love with you.'

'You kept it secret, so you obviously knew I wouldn't have liked it.'

'Yes, so I stopped doing it.'

'But you *started* doing it.'

I just couldn't believe it. It didn't fit with my idea of him at all. I saw him as a man without secrets, transparent – he seemed to say whatever was on his mind. How could someone talk so much and not be saying everything? Sometimes he seemed *too* honest. I wished he could learn to hold a little back; I didn't need to know *nearly* so much about the workings of his digestive tract. But perhaps the endless flow of speech was there to deflect, to make things seem one way whereas they were, in fact, another. He had been hosting this varmint, this *thing,* in our privileged space. It was like finding out he kept a rat in his pocket.

Up until that point I'd conceived of our relationship as something outlandishly pure, ring-fenced by an impenetrable barrier; we were utterly uncontaminated, germ-free, like a vacuum-packed surgical instrument. It was unthinkable that he could have kept a secret like this for three whole years.

'Who was she?'

'A journalist. I didn't really get on with her. We used to argue a lot.'

'So why did you shag her?'

'I don't know. Because she wanted to. I didn't know what *our* thing was going to turn into. I didn't know what you wanted from me.'

'And why did you tell me about it now?'

'Because she started texting again. I think she wants to be friends.'

'Oh, for Christ's sake.'

'She *is* kind of difficult.'

Harvey's insipid disparagement of her would incite me to ever greater rancour. She wasn't a moderately troubled human, she was a toxic leak, a swarm, a plague. She had single-handedly broken our borders, infiltrated our sentimental state.

'Fuck her. Fuck you.'

When I started to become insistent and unreasonable, Harvey would give up and try to wander off.

'Don't walk away!' I'd scream. 'Why can't you at least try to say something that makes it seem slightly better?'

I don't know what I imagined that might be. In order to do it he would have had to have made sense of so many other things: of love and hate and ties and threats and safety and mothers and fathers and insides and outsides. I don't see how he could have done it.

The result of the new knowledge was that, alongside loving Harvey, I also started to consciously loathe him. Anything I'd previously put to one side for the sake of harmony could no longer be ignored. His breath often smelled bad. He ate loudly. He had stupid ideas about gender. He liked shit TV shows. He didn't understand the first thing about women's clothes. If he was as truthful and dependable as I had previously imagined, none of this would have mattered. I could have continued to persuade myself that he was better than all the other people in the world, and that I must also be, by association. Instead, there was this filthy interloper wreaking havoc in our unblemished paradise. The cracks began to bifurcate.

With hindsight it seems ridiculous. Of course Harvey wasn't an angel, but somehow I'd let myself imagine he was in order to fall for him, to drop my defences, to allow us to become sealed in. I'd make-believed my love was indisputable, 'forgotten' that there could be anything else to it. From here it seems easy to see that to exalt someone so highly is delusional, a trick of the mind, an appalling act of stupidity. It makes me wonder about the hate that must have been there since day one. When I think back to our first date – his faintly sulphuric odour and megalomaniac conversational style – it seems clear: from the very beginning I'd needed to adore him in order to overcome my simultaneous aversion. The forces had to be perfectly balanced, binding me to him and him to me (goodness knows how he must have loathed me) in our unlikely and uncomfortable interrelation. That way we could withstand the hammer blows, the bullets; keep the good people in and the bad people out.

As it happened, the pressure it created inside the relationship was too great. Such a small thing in the end – hardly an infidelity, more a minor omission – but somehow, once the fractures had been activated, the love that had once looked so shiny and exquisite splintered spectacularly into dust. ■

Andrew McMillan

from the knotweed sonnets

When my boyfriend and I were buying our first house, the sale nearly fell through because there was Japanese knotweed in the garden. The bamboo canes seemed to be growing through everything, every document, every solicitors' meeting.

It's almost impossible to kill. Every few months a man in a red boiler suit turns up, tells us to get the animals inside, scorches the earth where it's grown, looks beneath shrubs, under hedgerows, for places it might have hidden itself. You treat it, cut down the dead sticks, burn them, but the roots remain; beneath the topsoil and the layers of muck, three metres deep, seven metres long, infiltrating the whole of the lawn and the flower beds.

Sometimes at night, both of us bound tight in our bed, I think I can hear it stretching, threatening to wake up, to grow through the walls.

sometimes I go out with an urge to hurt it
put my boot to the soft belly
of rotted stump   and the funghi   unkempt
sprung up from the mossy ground and flung
like scabs across the lawn   sometimes I need
the sound of something pulled up from the roots
and tossed aside   most days I'm out with loppers
to cut down the ambitions of the shrubs   when I
was in school there was a game   to throw
a punch as fast as you could and stop
an inch from someone's face   I tried it
once   with mum   tonight   in the dusk light
a final effort of the muscles   the snapping
crunching sound of something breaking

the neighbour says the old man has been dead
so long he's decomposed   no one can tell
what did for him in the end   the kid
over the road says he was murdered
hence the police car   parked as though guarding
someone of importance   a fortnight on
all the windows are open   the tongue
of the garage door rolled back   open mouth
full of boxes   the neighbour comes to say
he has two options for the cockerels
a blacked-out box so they never know dawn
and won't wake up   or else a collar
wrapped around their throat to stop their crowing
to break their necks if they try and scream

each evening I go out through the parched grass
to the raspberries and blackberries
reach through the netting to handle each one
in their swelling   ripe as the noses of drunks
I take them between my fingers
twist and pull   carry them back to the house
the neighbour spots me   he has a new trophy
a live-in lad to share the house with his mother
the neighbour walks him   topless and smiling   along
the path at the top of the gardens
he plays with the dog   he doesn't talk much
and I'm thinking of Pozzo   pulling
Lucky behind him   one moment dancing
the next moment mute   *it's like he's entangled*

the neighbour thinks someone is stealing
his chickens   that one has been left high
on a branch in warning   the neighbour
thinks a dog is after his chickens
or someone has trained a dog to steal
and a man is standing in the brook
with a sack   I sigh   say *rumour spreads
too quickly through this street*   another
neighbour asks if we've been growing weed
or if the other neighbours have
where is that smell coming from? they squeal
pulling up the floorboards one by one
weeks later   chicken heads like loose golf balls
in the woods   dog tracks in the early snow

sometimes my curiosity is a child
that wants to hunt things   like now   as I lever up
a square of the flagstone path   and find panic
a colony of ants   iron filings scattering
as they grab their small white eggs   and pupa
and their young   and run for cover underground
and in the midst of all their fizz and tumble
a family of translucent slugs
slowly rousing themselves from being curled in
on one another   they seem weary
and who can blame them   hiding from the world
and here I am   pulling off their roof   staring
as the ants carry off the ghosts of their future selves
and I close the lid of the path back down on them

                    the year of no touch   the garden shaggy
            and unkempt   autumn storms having turned leaves
                    to string   and that night you kissed me
                uncertain as drizzle   lips dewed and hungry
            and each time I think we've reached the edge of us
                    together – like that time in the middle
                of the Hope Valley   when I made up my mind
            to leave you   when the lit windows of each house
                        the train passed broke my heart
                it was lambing season late but barely dark
                    innocent marionettes in womb blood
            coming out into the night – each time like that
                we feel our way back   and coming home late
                    you greet me as though newly arrived

A Quarterly Attack Journal from Australia and the World

Winner of 2019 Stack Award for Best Original Non-Fiction

With cover art by **Michael Fikaris**, Issue 45 of The Lifted Brow includes: **Antonia Pont**'s tour-de-force 'hinking Feeling' column about the ethics and micro-dynamics of leadership; an exploratory essay om **Tess Pearson** that pieces together language and the body after pregnancy; **Odette Casamayor-isneros**, translated by **Erin Goodman**, with a story that peers through the screen and finds the other de wanting; plus an interview between author and translator on work, intimacy, and the soundtrack to it l; **Georgia Mill** elucidating the invisible but entrenched barriers to queer parenthood; **Kate Scardifield** ith an experimental essay on limbs, detachment, and the instinct to collect and categorise; an excerpt om **Eloise Grills**' upcoming Brow Books publication *big beautiful female theory*; punchy dystopic ction from **Kang Young-sook**, translated by **Janet Hong**, on contagion and the bonds that hold us; a rose poem from **Rosmarie Waldrop** that scrutinises semantics; poetry from **Georgia Kartas**, **Panda** /ong, and **Jason Phu**; and new comics and visual art by **Anya Davidson**, **Wakana Yamazaki**, **Mary** unig along with writing and art from many other superb writers and artists from Australia and the world.

THE LIFTED
BROW   thelistedbrow.com liftedbrow theliftedbrow

© JOEL STERNFELD
from *Walking the High line*

YOU ARE HERE, YOU ARE NOT A GHOST

Mark Doty

When I moved into my apartment twenty years ago, a few of the quasi-bohemians who'd bought their apartments when the building first went co-op lived here still. In the 1970s, when they moved into our five-story walk-up, Chelsea was considered dicey; nearly every lower-floor apartment's metal window gates were welded into place. They paid a few thousand dollars each, and if they ever had mortgages they paid them off long before I came along, and dwelled in a genteel poverty nearly impossible in Manhattan now. Pam, a therapist, saw clients in a parlor carved out of her dark 'floor-through', an apartment that occupies a whole story of a building, often with windows only in the front and the back. Her cats perched on the back of the sofa, or threaded the shadows beneath a long-untouched upright piano. She was president of the co-op for forty years, and from her first-floor peephole kept a sharp eye on comings and goings at the building's front door. When she announced in one of our regular meetings, 'If you have a visitor in the night, well, good for you, but PLEASE escort him out and make sure that door is locked behind him,' I knew it was me she was addressing. On the top floor lived Brian, a mostly out-of-work actor who went to auditions in an aging houndstooth jacket and a whiskey-toned fedora, trailing vapors of spirits and tobacco down the stairs behind him. If we met on the landing and stopped to talk a minute, he liked nothing better than to lower his voice to a stage whisper and make some camp and cutting remark about Pam. Sometimes I think I still hear his emphysemic ghost coughing, paused somewhere in the middle of the five flights up to his apartment, and some nights I sense Pam's phantom, disapproving eye fixed behind her old apartment's metal door.

If they linger here, they dwell beside three generations who've come after: middle-class owners like myself, then young residents whose parents have subsidized their down payments while they study opera or investment banking. Most recently a fellow who owns a pair of nightclubs bought two apartments, gutted them to the bricks and made a spacious duplex. The building's a palimpsest; remodelers found an old dumb waiter shaft that used to send food upstairs from the kitchen during the building's brief time as a single family home, then as an increasingly down-at-the-heels rooming house. Fallen plaster revealed a mysterious arched doorway that led into the building next door, for reasons no one knows. The whole place sags a little toward the spot where the original staircase was removed, and when I bought new shades to replace venetian blinds that must have been fixed in their position at least as long as Pam, I learned that each of my windows was a bit atilt, not one corner square.

For all its brawn and money, New York seems especially ephemeral. From its rough beginnings, it has staked its fortune on making itself new again, an ambitious, engaging monster whose nature is to grind up the wreckage of itself and toss up something new. At intervals along major avenues, the city has recently installed digital 'kiosks', a twenty-first-century version of a phone booth that indeed offers a phone without a booth one can use to call for help, a charging station, and, most prominently, a screen on either side offering ads, artwork, old photos, or trenchant observations on urban life, as if the city has decided to annotate its own sidewalks. The words or images change every thirty seconds or so, and I often near the end of a message just as the words dissolve into the next thing. But this one I read entire, a quotation from Colson Whitehead that appeared a few feet in the air above Eighth Avenue: *You are a New Yorker when what was there before is more real and solid than what is there now.*

What was there before in my neighborhood was a low skyline, buildings restricted to five stories save for those at the four corners of intersections, apartment towers from the 1920s and 30s that anchor the blocks with an elegant flourish. They end in step-backs to allow more light to reach the streets below. Height restrictions are gradually being overridden as developers want to push higher and produce enough units to cover the extravagant cost of construction, as well as ever more lavish penthouses. My little building contains just eight apartments; no one would build something that size now, unless the apartments were grand indeed.

I could narrate my neighborhood's relentless transformation, but you already know the story. Gone: Bright Food Shop, the Big Cup, Eighteenth & Eighth, David Barton Gym, Petite Abeille. The clothing shop of Raymond Dragon, a porn star and designer who made very small bathing suits. A shop that sold only striped French fabric. A ramen place on Sixth run by a group of very friendly young men who wanted you to like them, and made good soup, though they seemed to be playing the part of cafe staff in an extended, laddish prank. The Peruvian barber shop that trimmed my head for a decade, then became the office of a gelato parlor next door, and then a purveyor of rolled, unappealing slices of pizza, then nothing. The gelato place is gone too. *Nothing* is more common now than it used to be, since landlords learned they can ask for rent so high almost no one can pay it, then deduct the resultant losses of income from their taxes, engineering zones of absence that sometimes empty most of a block, and riddle even prosperous neighborhoods.

You can't attach memory or affection to vacancy. Though the shop was shuttered years ago, I remember distinctly the touch of the senior barber's hand on my neck, and the dark chocolate gelato flavored with the juice of mandarin oranges sold next door. I recall these gone places in details both sensory and intimate: a restaurant's warmth on a bitter night, or the startling apparition of a spotted fawn in my gym. A drag queen and her boyfriend, on the way back from upstate, had found the creature in the woods, and thought to rescue it, which it did not need, and now the hapless beauty stood on four skinny legs atop the front desk, utterly bewildered.

What was there before offered a rewarding sense of life in the particular: participation, comfort and strangeness. Perhaps if the old place engaged, startled or moved you, you're less likely to have such experiences with whatever has replaced it. It's often true that replacements are bland or uninteresting, as the local and particular are paved over by the corporate and general. What can Proustian imaginations do, after all, with nothing to work with but a sea of identical franchises?

In the random blur of cities we require allegiances. Loyalties make a place a home, and cannot shift as swiftly as the fevered economies of real estate. That barber shop has dimensionality to me, I can see and hear still the three barbers; I can re-enter the place imaginatively, down to the metal combs gleaming in jars of blue – alcohol? It is very difficult to do that with, say, any of the seemingly endless number of Duane Reades, where fluorescent lights bathe aisles of candy and makeup, and locked plexiglass cases of condoms and products to whiten the teeth. And it is impossible to enter into a full imaginative engagement with, and thus to remember, over many years, an empty storefront. What was there before will always be more real.

Vanished places are present to me, which is why I'm often not sure what's taken their place. Imagine mapping, on a computer screen, an atlas which would reveal the lost places beneath the now present. Suppose I could merge my maps with those of others: we'd be representing one thing this city really is, a shimmering hive, a vast structure of overlapping interiorities.

I used to get requests for donations from a group dedicated to the reclamation of a disused elevated train track that angled its way along the West Side all the way from the old railroad yards behind

Penn Station down to the warehouses and small former factories of the Meatpacking District and the far western edge of Chelsea near the Hudson. What made the tracks intriguing was the way they passed through the second stories of buildings, creating dreamy, unlikely passageways out of de Chirico, and second-story bridges between buildings that seemed like multiple New York versions of the Bridge of Sighs. The disused tracks were crumbling and weedy. I understood that this was a neighborhood effort to make a cozy park out of these odd spaces, so whenever they wrote I'd put ten dollars in an envelope and mail my contribution.

What was in the works was a long, narrow and elegant concourse, high enough above the street to freshen the air and perspective, low enough to make the view intimate, full of human detail. It would soon be considered one of the finest new urban spaces in the world. The world comes to see it; some days every third person on the sidewalk seems to carry a map. They stop randomly and turn the colored page, seeking orientation. Because I am often out walking with my dog, I am assumed to be local. Some ask me for directions in elegantly shaped English sentences; others say, hopefully, in one of the beautifully various accents of earth, 'Highline?'

The other inescapable new presence is Barneys, a sleek store that displays, across two rather sparsely stocked floors, clothing, accessories and jewelry priced at such an empyrean level that I am challenged to appreciate the allure of, say, a $1,000 pair of sneakers, a $5,000 purse. Small, sculptural pedestals suggest that what's for sale aspires to the condition of art, a sense reinforced by the floors' expanses of travertine. The space was Barneys decades ago, but by the time I moved here it had become a discount outlet, with wide circular racks of clothes bearing tags that indicated how the price declined with time, inviting customers to play an exasperating game: it might be cheaper if you wait, but it also might be gone.

I can see a corner of the store from my apartment window, and I liked following the grim old outlet's transformation. Above the newly enlarged windows and doors appeared an awning of stainless steel, delicately curved upward, and polished day after day until it gained the steely sheen of a spring sky verging on rain. Below it, they sheathed the front of the building in matte-black marble, which looked sensational until for some reason they tried to polish it. Much effort yielded a smeary, scumbled mess, the stone more and more obscured. Oddly, they put the jewelry department in a prominent corner, where big windows allowed a look inside from two directions. The cases inside contained bling you couldn't see from the street, maybe just a flash of a silver chain in halogen light, or the quick apparition of an aquamarine. These were the opposite of display windows; they announced the presence of something swathed, too precious for you on the sidewalk to even know what it was.

When the store first opened, the homeless used the beautiful awning as a shelter. They'd spread cardboard beds, boxes that hours before held subzero refrigerators or stoves or huge televisions. They would lie with their heads beside the glass and at least keep their upper bodies out of the rain. I often think of them, their bodies lined up along the sidewalks like stems laid parallel, the tops of their heads nearly touching the window glass. Did they know that a few feet from their skulls rested necklaces made of platinum, and jewels hung on chains so supple they felt liquid on the skin? How did the store ever banish them?

Barneys' troubles were in the news this summer, but word on the sidewalk had it our store would be saved. They painted on the windows, in tabloid letters that veiled the mannequins behind them, WE ARE NOT CLOSED and SPEND $ HERE. An announcement emerged from a hidden speaker, the kind of recorded female voice, both firm and calmly vacant, that might deliver instructions to be played in an emergency, or narrate a work of performance art. The first time I noticed it Seventh Avenue was crazy with sirens, so I could hardly make out a word. Then late at night, over a rising and fading rush of subway air through sidewalk grates, I heard it clearly.

I'd listen again, in a day or two, and understood it plainly as *We are not closing, we are still here.* What I heard that night was *You are not a ghost, you are still here,* as if Barneys would ever say such a thing.

The membrane between the living and the dead is generally understood – at least by daylight logic – to be permeable in one direction only. The living move into what Hamlet says is an 'undiscovered country, from whose bourn / No traveler returns'. But by the time the famous depressive speaks those words, he's already seen and heard his father's ghost, so he knows that versions of the departed do return – at Elsinore, at least, rather frequently. The body doesn't return, the whole self doesn't walk back into the daylight – but to be dead isn't to stop having a presence in the world. We engage every day with the language, ideas and belongings of the dead. A fiction-writing friend contends that the huge industry of yard sales, secondhand shops, flea markets and the like exists to manage the vast property of the dead, which otherwise might drown us in an awful, random tide.

There are a great many ways to be a ghost, or to partake of a quality of ghostliness.

Does it make you a little ghostly yourself, when what's gone is more present for you than what's here? The number of those who share your memory or affection will never increase. Who really wants to listen to the nostalgia of others? When I returned to Provincetown for the first time after I'd moved away, half the houses, every cafe and wedge of harbor view recalled a moment, an encounter with someone no longer living. It felt extraordinary to me, as though I walked through a full-sized version of a Renaissance memory palace, those structures built in the imagination to allow one to remember a complex argument or a long text by associating what one would see, walking through that dream-palace, with movements in the text. My memories – most often of people who were lost in the bitter crisis years of the epidemic – emerged with such force and clarity that I found myself describing them to the man I was with then, who soon had enough. He said, *Can't you be in the present?*

The answer was obvious. I felt flustered, and sorry if I were being rude to him, and at the same time put off; it wasn't rude, it wasn't my fault if the reanimated host of people I knew in those murderous hours were more vivid presences to me than my companion. He might have seen this as an opportunity to know me better, or might have found resonances in his own life, instead of complaining that my very real sorrow inhibited his holiday. I didn't articulate that at the time; I just tried, without much success, to keep my apparitions to myself.

G *host*, in the new digital landscape, has become a verb.
I met a man in his early forties, a striking, compact guy who'd recently moved to New York. One of his parents was from Jaipur, the other from Guatemala. He had the smooth confidence of the children of well-to-do exiles; educated, impeccably polite, he worked in corporate law. We met online. I went to his place, on the sixty-seventh floor of a new high-rise in Midtown; his furniture had not yet arrived, so there were only yoga mats and pillows on the floor. When he slipped out of his shirt and slacks, I was startled by the beauty of his body, supple and handsomely muscled, nothing showy or overdone about it, just the lean and rippling form of a man who looked a dozen years younger than he was, and seemed to wear his skin like a well-tailored suit in which he was supremely comfortable. And this man desired me? Ardently, it seemed. We had energetic, good-spirited sex on the floor beside a huge square window that faced west, so that we could look out, when we stopped to catch our breath, at shreds of clouds veiling the highest towers, the city gorgeous from that height, and riveting. Though that square panorama of my restless city didn't distract my attention from the liquid body I was lucky enough to lie beside for long.

We saw each other two more times. It was clear – I thought it was clear – that we were each interested in an unfolding erotic relation, and that nothing was expected beyond this pleasurable prospect. The second and third encounters were as lively and fresh as the first, and flavored too by what seemed the beginning of a friendship. I liked his sculptures, metal pieces he made as a relief from the meticulous focus of his work time; I liked talking with him, telling each other stories when we came up for air.

After our third time, at my place, he disappeared. I doubt anything terrible happened. He vanished from the hookup site on which we met; he might have canceled his membership, or might simply have blocked me so that I would no longer see his profile. He seemed to have blocked my phone number so I couldn't call or text. Gone as if he'd never been there. I was startled that I spent so much time wondering why. I wasn't in love with him. I had lost nothing but a still-tentative friendship, which was only a few weeks old. Why did I feel so hurt?

The absence of an explanation, the fact of no knowable cause left me with a kind of gap, something I'd keep revisiting. He absented himself for a reason I have no means of knowing, so of course I imagine reasons: had he wanted a kind of relationship with me that I wasn't available for? Was it age difference; would his family or friends question why he had a sixty-six-year-old friend? Did he decide to go back to an old partner? Had I said or done something to offend?

No amount of this sort of thinking avails. The blank space where my understanding of his motive should be is likely a permanent one. Had he said why he was disappearing, I would likely have forgotten about it in a little while. But like most ghosts, he said nothing, and the story persists in memory because it has no satisfying outcome.

No wonder this behavior's called *ghosting*. I read reports on a study of children who'd lost friends this way, and maybe for other reasons as well. Doctors found the children's pain at the loss of their companions was physical; you could treat it with aspirin. An absence you can explain is one thing; to be even a little haunted by what you can't know is an oddly persistent feeling with a different sort of ache to it.

A young woman on my block pauses on the sidewalk, a few feet from the corner where I'm waiting for the walk sign, phone held to her ear. She steps off the curb, as though she's just heard something so incredulous that she has to quit the flow of pedestrians to respond. 'You're not listening to me,' she says.

And then, 'You're *not* listening to me.'

Then, 'You're not *listening* to me.' Pause. 'You're not listening to me.' One more time, the fifth, this time the whole phrase louder.

Then, 'Why should I listen to you?' Not once, but five times.

Then, 'You don't get what I'm saying,' five times.

It's around the second set of repetitions that I think, who would listen to this? No one, of course, there's no one on the other end of the line, no other end, probably no line. The young woman's frantic, enraged performance is so ritualized that it might be an assignment from her acting class, or a social experiment. The strict pattern makes her easy to spot. But in truth I encounter someone doing more or less this on the street almost every day, with spontaneity or its semblance, with conviction or what resembles it. Sometimes they shout into one of the remaining pay phones, and thus give themselves away by using machines everyone knows don't work. But the shouting itself reveals their game: we are the audience, and the goal of the speaker is to tell, without apology or consideration, the endless litany of reprehensible things that you, you, you did to ME. Sometimes that's a refrain: I can't believe you did this to ME.

No one on the street is expected to respond; the lamenting or raging 'caller' is a desperate, hungry ghost, wheeling her monologue through sometimes startled but permanently indifferent streets.

My dog Ned and I wait at the corner on Ninth Avenue for the light to change. In that barely conscious way one does in the city, we take note – we both take note – of the man who's walking in our direction, his spiky beard and hair like charcoal lines drawn on his face and skull to express his interior field of crackling electricity. He's striding forward muttering in the direction of whatever it is his eyes are fixed on, something that is and isn't there, and immediately I'm thinking of that famous and dazzling outdoor sculpture in New Mexico, *The Lightning Field*, a stretch of desert set with metal towers intended to attract lightning. That's what this guy is carrying in his body, a lightning field.

He isn't close enough to touch us or to lunge at us, though he will be. I don't want him to know I'm looking at him, so I turn my face back to the crosswalk and the walk sign as if my gaze could make it change. Ned turns with me, a little nervously, to face the street. I wonder if I should walk right out into the street, against the light, but it would be obvious that I was trying to get away from him.

While I'm weighing this, he screams. A shriek, really, that seems it could tear the morning open; the phrase I think of is Hart Crane's: *A rip-tooth of the sky's acetylene.* As if the fabric of the day, the collectively constructed sense that we're all more or less all right, has been just a painted canvas, and his scream is the blade that has hacked the flimsy thing right down the middle.

I can't keep myself separate from it. For a moment, a moment only, I tell myself I'm not him, his scream isn't mine, nor his fury, or his inability to do anything but scream like a mortally wounded creature on the sunny Eighth Avenue sidewalk. The walk light's green, ordinary things require my attention. I have a dog to walk.

Our fear of ghosts, thought Lafcadio Hearn, isn't so much of seeing or hearing them; the terrible thing is they might touch us.

If what's vanished is more real than what remains, then what's gone is a kind of extension of the self, a city of the self, since what has disappeared exists now only in memory. And memory – not history but private memory, associative, metonymic, saturated in feeling – lives only within the head or the spine, or the cells. And in books. C.P. Cavafy speaks to his hometown of Alexandria, in Edmund Keeley's translation, with extraordinary intimacy:

> I created you while I was happy, while I was sad,
> with so many incidents, so many details.

> And, for me, the whole of you has been transformed into
>   feeling.

The powers that seem to steer the course of our lives in the twenty-first century thus far also want to build impressive, technically marvelous means of recreating experience, but their aim is to sell to us not only devices but the sort of lives they imagine for us. New York seems a premier proving ground for such experiments. Times Square, formerly a kind of sexual agora of old movie houses, video arcades, boothstores and strip clubs where people, mostly men, could meet in spaces that largely took down barriers of class, race and respectability to allow a kind of free zone for Eros: seedy, sometimes liberating, not infrequently awful, though what was dispiriting about the scene was also pungent: here the wraps came off the culture's weirdly contradictory and barely articulated desires.

Gone, of course, all that, and workers in uniform hired to sweep up, and cops hustling away anyone who tries to revive an old shell game or trick passersby with some ancient scam of a card game. The funny thing is that it doesn't feel cleaned up; it's crowded and ugly and the tourist hordes seem to carry a restless anger in their chests, even if they're not aware of it.

Because there's nothing there. Nothing to see. Just the blazing lights of huge screens advertising TV shows, movies, devices, stylish goods with the manufactured aura of 'luxury' about them. The light of these enormous images seems to hang in the air over the streets, blending into a kind of unfamiliar presence. Or not unfamiliar; it's the light of car lots at night, blazing mercury lamps intended to reveal any kind of movement, or the light of office buildings, left on for the men and women who empty trash cans and polish floors. The light is so pervasive you can take pictures anywhere, using one of the devices hawked on the big dreamy screens up above. That's what people do, the poor more or less local kids who've taken the train down from the Bronx, the white kids who've come in from New Jersey, the tourists from everywhere, everyone moving in their packs: they take pictures, many posted there and then on Instagram. They pose dramatically or flirtatiously, postures they already know how to assume without embarrassment, fulfilling their parts in a place that is nowhere, despite the expensive souvenirs.

The beautiful Highline reworks the artifacts of industry into a series of viewing points, picturesque stops along a path. Down there, where they made leather goods or automotive mirrors, or worked marble into thresholds and basins, those are galleries now, and further south, the lockers, where the meat was hung to age, are torn down for condominiums, and the door to a club where men used to strip naked and writhe against each other in a dim red light – *Reader, I have haunted these corridors myself, I slipped down their throats like a thief, I married them, and I am not dead, as so many are, though I am a ghost* – that door now leads, I am not making this up, to the boutique of Christian Dior. One becomes a phantom when what you remember is more real than what is, or one becomes a phantom when what you are is yearning for those invisible qualities that are suggested by an object that does not in itself possess them. This hat, these shoes, these gloves are gestures in the direction of a life held up as desirable. Bring them home and unwrap them from the handsome boxes and tissue in which they have been presented to you, what do you have? The moment of unboxing is so full of promise, so enviable that we record it in videos logged, stored, there for anyone to see. Barneys is closing and everything's 50 percent off. A steal, to pick up a $4,000 tote bag for $2,000! It's as if the old discount place has re-emerged, come back from beneath the seashell curve of the spiral stair. Racks of marked-down stuff, whatever glamour the place could boast gone. They pay people to walk up and down the avenue wearing sandwich boards, some illuminated, reading STORE CLOSING. The sign bearers are supposed to pass out flyers that no one wants; I've seen one exasperated worker simply throw her pile in the trash. And half another's sandwich board thrown down, discarded, an obstacle to anyone walking tonight's damp sidewalk.

My dearest friend will say, after he's lamented something that troubles him, 'First World problems.' A handy bit of shorthand, that: he deflates his own importance, relativizes his difficulty, stands at an ironic bit of distance, and is ready to move on. The people who

shout into phones, performing rage or misery, the men who fume or
scream on the street, the homeless couple camped behind the steel
supports of scaffolding between the Seventh Avenue sidewalk and
the oversize windows of Starbucks, with their boxes and blankets
and their dog. (Imagine sleeping, as they are this cold late morning,
between those two audiences.) Not ready to move on, any of them.
Me either, sometimes. At the end of a day in New York City one
might stop to consider the great stream of faces that have passed by
us on that day, how many of those never or only barely registered,
and which ones are still inscribed in us. The city places us in relation
to one another, then both underscores and erases those connections.
Just a few from today: my homeless friend, a kind and weary black
woman, hurried across Seventh Avenue to ask me for money, calling
my name from halfway across, and I had to wave her off because I
was late for a session with my trainer at the gym. The two well-spoken
kids who stopped on the street to pet Ned; the boy recited facts about
golden retrievers in the somewhat puffed-up way of children who
have accumulated knowledge they will someday need, and I was
entirely charmed. The heavy man on the train, surrounded with what
I guess were his worldly goods, who fixed his attention solely on me
and shouted, halfway down the car, YOU CAN SUCK MY DICK.
A small community of sparrows, in a leafless shrub in Union Square,
leaping from branch to branch like random thoughts.

At this point in history, in America at least, even minor connections
between people are endangered. The kind of simple interactions that
form an essential social fabric allow one's perceptions to be validated
or challenged, and collectively enable something like consensus, a
reasonably accurate understanding of what's going on. We're less
likely to speak to strangers; you don't know what you might be
starting. The small businesses where I actually recognized or knew
owners or clerks are mostly gone, some replaced by franchises whose
employees travel hours to get here and don't know the neighborhood,
and don't tend to keep those jobs for long. The devices that are
supposed to bring us together do so, with chosen groups of the like-

minded. But they also make us more alone, as we form connections that are easily broken, or fall under the spell of a singular viewpoint. It's difficult to become a white supremacist or a jihadist on your own. How would you sustain it? But if you have an internet connection you can be alone and find like-minded souls, however dark they may be. Or you can use the rich array of world-shifting electronics to take the expected pictures of yourself and your friends in photographable places, and post them online as we do, having purchased what was, before the last two decades or so, usually free: memory, visibility, a feeling of legitimacy, a sense of being real to ourselves.

But 'the world is wily', as the poet Susan Mitchell writes in a poem in her book *Rapture*, 'and doesn't want to be caught'. Nor does it want to be theorized; the city's too big, too inclusive and random to submit to singular interpretations. As much as the attention-grabbing power of the virtual and the glittering net of capital can feel seamless here, encompassing, I love this city for its insistence on allowing for the anarchic and the genuine. Something is always breaking through, if only in some momentary constellation of meanings, or in some unmistakably human gesture that spills out and for a while transforms the climate of whoever receives it. The most powerful of these are almost inevitably the ones not particularly meant for you; they arrive, as joy mostly does, out of nowhere.

I don't think ghosts experience joy; they hover with their faces turned toward the past, and cannot attend wholly to the moment in which something might revivify them. Most living people become ghosts for a while. The trick to spending less time as a phantom is to give attention *to* attention, aware of your physical self now, alert to whatever arises in this moment and the shining edge of the next sliding into view.

Or sometimes you just have to be tired, and not preoccupied, and caught off guard. As I was, a few nights ago in Penn Station. That underground, unwindowed, unloved place is a hall of doom after dark, the commuter hordes gone, whatever cheer that might have been generated by their eagerness to get home, their beers and bags of popcorn, their shouted 'good nights' all dissipated now. There are a few guards, a few police officers, sometimes armed soldiers in desert-colored fatigues, and then there's everyone who lives here, or tries to. Some sleep on the floor, some stand awkwardly in the corridors, asking for help or muttering private litanies. Always the same awful encounter with what you can't begin to change, with pain and need you can't ever address. I'd come from a dinner with friends in New Jersey, and wearily made my way toward the A train. When I came to the wide descending hallway that leads to the turnstiles, the air filled with a dense, brassy music, confident and driving, a great propulsive swing to it. Half hidden behind a column, a man sat on a high wooden stool, body wrapped around the long golden shape of the saxophone he played with a superbly controlled abandon. No one in the corridor but me, and his music swelled like a warm golden current. I recognized the tune, though I couldn't name it – an upbeat jazz standard, something from a musical? It didn't matter; it was a song about the will and nerve to go forward, to walk out into the night with the sure knowledge that more awaited you than exhaustion and loss. There is in us, the music said, refusal, will, momentum, joy. I was startled by what it called to mind – the watercolored drawings I'd seen weeks before in London, elongated women and men veiled and rayed in warm yellows, layers of golden light: the human form divine. Halfway down the corridor I turned back, walked to where the musician sat and dropped the two dollars I had into the open instrument case at his feet. He didn't look up or otherwise acknowledge me. Maybe a very slight tip of the head? Either he didn't care or was pouring himself entirely into those passages, making a corridor of his own out of this burnished splendor made with his own breath. A corridor I walked down, all the way to the A, and felt warmed by even after the doors of the train car closed. ∎

NATION

Sorry, the coastline is closed today, but we can accommodate
you offshore. Our stevedores will help carry your belongings.
This way please for a complimentary spray of DDT. No jewels
allowed in quarantine, leave them with me, but when you're free,
we'll give you a house with a chain-link fence, an orange grove
and an AK-47. Forget where you came from, forget history.
It never happened, OK? We need soldiers on the front line.
Of course we can coexist. We say potato, they say potato.
We give them their own ghetto. Listen, sometimes you need
to dance with whoever is on the dance floor, which means,
sometimes you need to drive large numbers of their people
in a truck across the dark. A few may die, but then ask,
If I'm not for me, who is? It's absolutely forbidden to touch
the women's knickers. If things go awry (shit happens),
better to dump their bodies in the desert. No drowning allowed
on international TV. No talking about jasmine-scented streets
either. Understand friend, the conscience is a delicate broth.
Sometimes it feels good to be bad. Step over this field of bones.
Here's where the wall is going to go. If you're not happy,
you can leave, but tell the world we're building a new country.
Entry is free and we welcome all!

© JULIE MEHRETU
Mogamma (A Painting in Four Parts): Part 2, 2012
Courtesy of the artist, Marian Goodman Gallery and White Cube

DIMINISHING RETURNS

Fatin Abbas

T here had been a river here a month before. A full-blooded river jolting over rocks, rippling with currents, swooshing around bank bends. Now there was no river. Just an arid depression, not even a hint of moisture to suggest that there had ever been water here.

'Where is it?' asked Alex.

His translator, William, a Nilote from the area, stood beside him, gazing at a bank which had been green when they'd first driven through shortly after Alex's arrival in Saraaya. They were sixty kilometers north of town, here to survey one of the main grazing thoroughfares through which the nomads passed on their way south.

'It's gone,' said William.

'Gone?'

'I guess it dried up already.'

'And when will it come back?'

'Next July maybe.'

'Maybe?'

'It used to come back every wet season, but the last few years, it's so-so. Sometimes it comes, sometimes it doesn't.'

Alex turned back to the landscape. A scene that overwhelmed and underwhelmed all at once with its spectacular monotony. Blank slate of a bleached sky. Flat land stretching around him. Clumps of desiccated trees to the east. In the far distance, a man sitting atop a camel wound his way from nowhere to nowhere. Alex had been sent to this remote district between north and south Sudan to update maps. It was an information-gathering project run by an American NGO based in the capital, Khartoum, nine hundred kilometers to the north. The maps in use by the local authorities were out of date – a new map was needed to help the organization tailor and deliver aid to the district. Alex had been hired from America to do the job. He'd landed in Saraaya at the turn of the new millennium to find hostilities between southern rebels and northern government simmering in the background.

After authorization for his map had finally arrived the week before, he had set about his work in earnest. Trailed by William, he'd zipped around the district with his measuring rope and his surveying telescope and his satellite devices, pouncing on unsuspecting passersby in the market to ask about farms and roads and grazing routes; traveling to villages and water wells and nomads' camps in the plains on the peripheries of town. He and William had undertaken expeditions to the sandy plains of the goz to the north, which stretched from Chad to the White Nile. Great tracts of flat semi-desert unfurling as far as the eye could see, short, dry trees dotting the landscape here and there.

They had driven south, to the enormous wetland terrain of the Sudd, a carpet of marshes and swamps and bogs with islands of floating reeds as vast as football fields, feeding into the White Nile that flowed toward Khartoum. They had explored the network of rivers between these two terrains, life source of nomads and Nilotes, irrigating crops, nourishing livestock and people.

But the more Alex studied the landscape – squinting over his maps by night and gathering information during his expeditions by day – the more confused he became. He had never dealt with a geography like this before. It confounded everything he knew about natural habitats, land formations, water systems. He was used to landscapes changing slowly, in minuscule increments, over years of soil erosion, the weathering of rock layers, the creep of vegetation.

But here, from one season to the next, the landscape changed completely. During the rainy season swamps and rivers and lakes materialized, only to disappear entirely during the dry season and reappear in different places with the following rains. A river twenty meters wide that gushed with torrential water dwindled to a pathetic dribbling stream three months later, or dried up altogether, as this one had. Desert turned into lush, rolling grassland between May and November, only to turn back into desert during the dry season. Nomadic settlements sprung up with their rickety reed houses and cattle and camels in one place only to be packed up soon after. Even the town, Saraaya, was in a continuous state of upheaval. It had been destroyed three times during the war. Each time it was rebuilt – after people returned, dragging behind them their diminished belongings – things changed. Streets shifted. Families invaded each other's compounds. Land which belonged to one person was suddenly farmed by someone else. The market disappeared, reduced to skeletal bones of burnt-out stalls, only to spring up elsewhere, with all the hustle and bustle of trade. Everything – villages and rivers and grazing routes – had two names, one in Arabic, and one in Nilotic, so that he found himself having to cope with the confusion not only of multiple languages, but also of multiple place names.

One map, he realized now, would not be enough. He had to make two. One depicting dry-season geography and one the wet-season landscape. Even then, he knew that within six or seven years the maps would again have to be updated. Once rivers shifted their courses the meander lines would have to be redrawn; new grazing routes would have to be shaded in, new swamps, new deserts spreading south with diminishing rains.

He had little time to finish the work – only four weeks to present something to his boss Greg, who'd been calling from Khartoum to check on his progress. Alex had started late. Authorization for the map had been held up by the troubles in the district. Southern rebels and the northern government were at each other's throats in a war that had been ongoing since independence in '56. And Saraaya, along with its oil fields, was right in the middle of it. Whoever controlled the district controlled the oil. Right now it was the government.

After his last phone call with Greg, in which his boss had exhorted him to get going quickly or else, Alex had asked William to arrange a meeting with Nilote and nomad elders. Three days later they'd arrived to find a large group collected in a clearing on the edge of town, under a tree whose branches were still verdant at the end of the rainy season. Men and women and children sat on straw mats on the grass. Light darted and leapt from face to face. Alex stood nervously before the unabashed gaze of the congregation, branches above him swaying with a breeze that stirred the heat into life rather than dispersed it.

He hadn't expected so many people to show up. William had arranged for him to meet a handful of elders, but word had gotten out about the meeting, and he'd found bodies and faces packed under the shade, looking back at him expectantly. Being the only white man for miles around meant that he drew a crowd.

Turning to William, he said, 'Can you ask them to introduce themselves first?'

One of the Nilote elders – a man with drooping eyelids and milky irises and wearing a red beret angled jauntily on his head – spoke. William translated. The elder wanted, first, to hear from Alex. What was America like? Did he like Saraaya?

The next ten minutes were lost to chitchat. Growing impatient, Alex told William to ask about the boundaries.

'They will answer your questions, so you must show them the same courtesy.'

Alex felt the precariousness of the balance of power he shared with his translator, who was really the one in control of things, and he was compelled to oblige him by answering more questions from the crowd.

Finally they returned to the business at hand. William translated as Alex, pointing to a map pinned and fluttering against the tree, tried to explain what he wanted to know. An old woman in a blue dress yawned. Three children fidgeted at the front. A man in a jellabiah scratched his arm. A little girl sucked her thumb. He rushed on.

'Tell them I'm meeting with them to determine the boundary between Nilote farms and nomad grazing lands,' he said. 'Ask if any elders would like to speak to the matter.'

William translated. The same Nilote elder rose, propping himself up on his stick. He pointed to the horizon. The boundary, he said, was clear. Since the time of his forefathers there had been an understanding that when the nomads arrived in Saraaya at the end of the rains each year, they could graze their cattle north of the bend of the River Kinu, at a village about one day's walk from the town. Their grazing land stretched from that bend up to the gum-tree forest. The nomads who had lost their herds in the droughts and settled in Saraaya cultivated farmland in that stretch. Down from Saraaya to Agok was Nilote grazing land, and from Saraaya to the savannahs was Nilot farmland.

Murmurs of assent rippled through the crowd. But then a nomad elder stood up. The jellabiah he wore was a bright white, brighter than those worn by the men sitting with him, a turban wrapped neatly above a high brow and small eyes and a thick, graying mustache.

It's true, he began, that back in the time of their forefathers, the nomads grazed north of the river bend. But that was long ago. Before the war. Before the droughts. Back in the time of the English. Things had changed since then. Grazing routes had shifted with lessening rains, war had scattered people. Many of the nomads had settled to farm, many of the Nilotes had moved south to join their kinsmen beyond the savannahs. The land boundaries were different now.

When he spoke again, there was an explosion of movement. People sprang to their feet. Babies crawling on the ground and little boys and girls hovering around the circle stopped what they were doing to stare at their agitated parents in surprise.

'What did he say?'

'He's saying the nomads' land stretches from Saraaya up to the gum-tree forest.' William's finger traveled from the black dot of the town on the map up to a gray-shaded area, about thirty kilometers north west, indicating the forest. 'He's claiming half the land the Nilotes say is theirs as grazing pasture for the nomads.'

Shoes and sticks rose in the air. Turbans unspooled to the ground. Heads and hands and legs were suddenly locked in a jumble. From the sidelines, women urged on their menfolk. William plunged into the circle to pull people apart. Alex too pushed his way in. Immediately someone's elbow landed in his cheek, and he stumbled out, eyes watering from pain.

That was the first meeting. He arranged meetings with each group separately, but the map of nomad grazing routes then conflicted with the map of Nilote grazing routes. Same went for the farmlands. He hadn't even figured out the district boundaries yet, and there were still field trips to be taken, long days of compiling information – correlation of Arabic and Nilotic names of rivers, lakes, villages; cross-checking findings with the authorities; entering data into his blueprint map.

Each day brought more doubts and questions. It wasn't just that he was thwarted at every turn, or that his measuring instruments were useless in the face of boundaries as difficult to grasp as smoke. The war too was taking its toll. The rebels inching closer to the district cast a cloud of peril over the map. He'd begun having nightmares in which he was lost in a maze of mud walls, chased by faceless armed men, unable to find his way out; in another dream he was trapped in a vault packed from floor to ceiling with maps; maps weighing on his chest and arms and legs and maps in his mouth.

And now, as though in a dream, this river that had disappeared. He stared out at the smooth parched depression at his feet.

'How long will this take?' William asked, glancing down at his watch. 'I promised to drive Layla home today.'

Alex sighed. Another date with Layla, the cook at the compound. Alex had been clued into the romance by Dina, with whom he shared the compound in town. Dina had explained, the day of Layla's return – when William had abruptly marched off to the kitchen to speak to her – that she and Alex needed to give William and Layla more room to be alone. A few days later, during one of their field trips, William confessed that he and Layla were 'getting to know one another'.

Alex was happy for William. It was sweet how he and Layla huddled together in the kitchen. The little presents which William picked up for her when he was out and about with Alex – a beaded necklace, or a silver bracelet – which Alex was invariably asked to give his opinion on, in William's quest to identify Layla's tastes and preferences, to please her by surprising her.

But the courtship was interfering with work. William was slow to leave the compound when Layla was in. And, when he and Alex were out on one of their expeditions, he was always impatient to return. No matter how often Alex explained to William the intricacies of mapping – yes, he had to map all the grazing routes, and yes, it was necessary to document precise coordinates of water wells in the district, which meant that they did, indeed, have to travel to all of them – William didn't get it. The long drives, the hours spent fiddling with equipment, the mindless waiting were all great chunks of time that it was clear he'd rather be spending with Layla.

'We just got here,' said Alex.

They had been delayed leaving because first, there had been a problem with the truck tire, which had to be replaced. That had taken up all morning. By the time the tire was fixed, it was lunchtime. Alex had wanted to head out anyway, but William insisted on staying and having lunch at the compound. 'We should have left earlier. You wanted to stay because of Layla.'

It was the first time he was voicing objection to the amount of time William was spending with her.

William's eyes narrowed.

'So now I'm not entitled to my lunch break?'

'I'm just saying,' said Alex, 'I want to finish as soon as possible too, but I need an hour.'

'It's the end of the day.'

'It takes –' Alex stopped. It was pointless. They were both frustrated, and getting nowhere. 'Right now we're wasting time. Let me just get on with it, okay? The sooner I start, the sooner we can get back.'

William folded his arms and stared imperiously out over the riverbed.

Alex walked back to the truck. A gust of wind filled his ears with noise, lashed dust against his calves. Shrubs in the distance bent their branches one way and then the other. He squinted to keep dirt out of his eyes. He pulled out surveying equipment from the bed of the truck as William crouched by the bank, whipping at sand with a supple branch he'd picked up somewhere.

'Are you coming to help or what?' Alex called, stacking boxes on top of one another.

William rose and threw the branch away. Took more time than was necessary dusting off his trousers. Finally came over to the car, lifted equipment out.

Alex walked back to the bank and dropped the boxes on the ground. He looked out at the river which had ceased to be a river, a river which might or might not become one again next year, and wondered how, on earth, he was to find his bearings. ∎

The magazine of Chatham House covering international affairs
A resource for governments, businesses and academics since 1945
Fresh thinking on the way the world is run and how to improve it

The World Today

Subscribe today and stay informed

theworldtoday.org   +44 (0)20 3544 9725

A composite image of every piece of spatial analysis conducted by Forensic Architecture
and Amnesty International in relation to the bombing of Rafah, Gaza, on 1 August 2014.

CRIMES OF SPACE

Eyal Weizman

in conversation with Rana Dasgupta

RANA DASGUPTA: I'd like to begin by talking about the *shape* of the border, which conventionally appears as a line.

Because of its particular conception of threat – external and internal – Israel has made a disproportionate contribution to state theories of defence and segregation. In *Hollow Land* (2007), your account of the military, bureaucratic and architectural systems with which the Israeli state organises territories and peoples, you identify a remarkable moment in its evolving conception of 'border'. You describe the debate surrounding the Bar Lev Line: a chain of fortifications constructed by Israel along the Suez Canal after the 1967 Arab–Israeli War. The Bar Lev Line was supposed to be impregnable, but during the Yom Kippur War of 1973 it was breached in two hours by the Egyptian army.

This defensive disaster enhanced the influence of Ariel Sharon, principal critic of the Bar Lev Line, who had dismissed it as the Israeli 'Maginot Line' – referring to the vast defensive barrier built by France in the 1930s to protect against German invasion. Sharon argued that the border should be thought of not as a line but as a network extending deep into Israeli territory. You summarise his reasoning thus:

> If the principle of linear defence is to prohibit (or inhibit) the enemy from gaining a foothold beyond it, when the line is breached at a single location – much like a leaking bucket of water – it is rendered useless. A network defence, on the other hand, is flexible. If one or more of its strongpoints is attacked and captured, the system can adapt itself by forming new connections across its depth.

EYAL WEIZMAN: It is fair to say that there has never been an agreed-upon boundary to Israel and its territorial ambitions.

When the Zionist leadership accepted the territories marked out for Israel under the UN Partition Plan in 1947, they expected the borders to change during the anticipated Arab–Israeli War, which was already in preparation. Even after the war, and the expulsion of the Palestinians from Israel's territorial acquisitions, Israeli historians have reported that the prime minister, David Ben-Gurion, accepted the ceasefire agreement because he imagined the borders would be further extended during the next round of conflict.

Still today, the question of borders has not been resolved. There is no consensus within Israel about whether a Palestinian state should exist – even in the most minimal of ways – and so there can be no agreement about Israel's eastern border. Instead, there is the contested frontier along the West Bank governed by military forces, a compliant Palestinian authority and settler groups that dictate the political agenda.

In the absence of any hard or durable state boundary, smaller manifestations of borders, or border devices, have sprung up everywhere. Like worms cut into pieces, each taking on renewed life, fragments of the border exist deep within the space under Israeli control. In the West Bank, we see this represented by the fences around settlements and military bases, and by important infrastructure such as roads and bridges that function as methods of segregation. And we see it, of course, in the wall itself, which twists through Palestinian lands.

In Gaza, the wall has a different function. It not only cuts the territory off from the rest of Palestine but, by controlling land and maritime borders of the Gaza envelope, Israel is also able to regulate the quantities of all resources entering the territory: electricity, food, medicine, petrol, building materials and so on. With the ability to starve Gaza of resources, Israel ensures the Strip's total dependency.

It is in this context that we need to see the so-called 'Trump Plan', which would create a Palestinian state by connecting fragments of land around Palestinian towns and cities through a network of raised highways, tunnels and bridges. The result would be two mutually exclusive geographies superimposed over the same land. This amounts to the vertical partitioning of Palestine, with Israelis travelling by bridge over Palestinian areas, owning the water underneath and controlling the airspace above – something I have called a 'politics of verticality'.

There are many borders, and each one produces a different kind of territorial scenario and governing apparatus. The absence of a single line around the state has meant that the border is everywhere. And it goes beyond the organisation of physical space. The border provides a structure to state institutions and bureaucracies based on permits and the control of circulation – who can enter where and when.

DASGUPTA: What does it mean for a border to exist within a bureaucracy?

WEIZMAN: Let's say you're a Palestinian in the West Bank. The wall that runs through the territory requires you to conform to a regime of permits that controls every aspect of your movement. You need a permit to pass through the checkpoints, and in order to obtain it you will need to do various things, including, sometimes, collaborating with the security forces. There are different kinds of permits, allowing movement at different times, for different durations and to different places in Israel, so that your movement in space is continuously and transparently monitored. In order to enforce this permit regime, the state must

In July 2015, Forensic Architecture completed an investigation into the bombing of Rafah, Gaza, on 1 August 2014. Denied entry into the Gaza strip, Amnesty International and Forensic Architecture relied on thousands of images and videos shared online, or sent to them directly by citizens and journalists.

Forensic Architecture located photographs and videos within a 3D
model to tell the story of one of the heaviest days of bombardment
in the 2014 Israel-Gaza war. 'The Image-Complex', Rafah, Gaza.
© FORENSIC ARCHITECTURE, 2015

Video still showing two bombs in mid-air fractions of a second before
impact in the Al Tannur neighbourhood in Rafah, Gaza, on 1 August 2014.
© FORENSIC ARCHITECTURE, 2015

maintain constant individual surveillance, optical and technical.

The concrete and razor wire of the West Bank wall are reinforced with highly effective electronic sensors, a form of smart-fencing technology at which Israel excels. Border control has become one of Israel's most important export industries. But we need to think of the border not only as a physical instrument but also as an optical-bureaucratic apparatus.

DASGUPTA: What has changed since you wrote *Hollow Land*?

WEIZMAN: The most important change since the early 2000s is the advent of digital surveillance. Surveillance complements the physical apparatus of the border rather than replacing it. Surveillance has moved into licence-plate and facial recognition, social networks and digital communication. Civil society and human rights activists in Palestine are monitored through their WhatsApp messages. An Israeli company called NSO Group Technologies is at the forefront of cyber surveillance and it has been reported that its product, Pegasus spyware, now aids repressive regimes worldwide. People are being arrested for what they post on Facebook. So again, we are talking about a system that is both physical and digital, and the intricacies of the relationship between the physical and the digital have very much become manifest since *Hollow Land* was written.

DASGUPTA: For several regimes across the world, Israel provides a kind of security gold standard. To what extent are its techniques copied and exported elsewhere?

WEIZMAN: It follows a circular movement. Israel has had very good European tutors when it comes to colonial technologies of domination. The logic of surveillance, segregation and separation is colonial in nature; it also existed in Palestine under British Mandate between the First and Second World Wars, before the Israeli state was formed. This same approach was applied in apartheid South Africa, where borders of

Forensic Architecture has investigated the use of live ammunition by Israeli security forces in 2018 protests in Gaza. On 1 June 2018, a shot fired into a group of Palestinian protestors near the village of Khuzaa killed twenty-one-year-old volunteer medic Rouzan al-Najjar and injured two others.

Forensic Architecture's model captures the moment after the fatal shot is fired.
© FORENSIC ARCHITECTURE, 2019

From the positions of the three medics, who were struck by the same bullet, a 'cone of fire' can be estimated, from within which the bullet must have travelled.
© FORENSIC ARCHITECTURE, 2019

every kind were, once again, used as instruments of population control.

Israel has operated under this logic for so long that it has developed many technologies of surveillance and physical domination, which, in turn, have been adopted by like-minded governments such as India (in particular along its frontier with Pakistan) and the US.

Europe is now at the forefront of this border frenzy. One thousand kilometres of security wall have been built in Europe since the fall of the Berlin Wall in 1989, some by agencies like Frontex – the European Border and Coast Guard Agency – with the specific intention of controlling migration. Walls and fences are only the most visible part of the system. Surveillance and control throughout the depth of the territory are crucial corollaries. For example, I think that the political contradictions imposed by Brexit on the new Irish border will make it an important test case for how borders of the twenty-first and twenty-second centuries will operate.

DASGUPTA: What is the justification for such a system in Europe?

WEIZMAN: In the early 2000s, of course, it was the 'war on terror'. Post-9/11, the fear of 'terror' accustomed populations to the idea that state surveillance is benign, or that it is designed to serve their security and safety. I cannot overemphasise the psychological impact of this ambient terror on a population – and I don't mean just the actions of terror groups but also the way that those actions were amplified in the public domain by governments and the media.

But this security-based rationale has since morphed into a rationale focused on anti-migration, which is now prevalent throughout Europe. It has been the basis for an extremely invasive surveillance regime, which attempts to control the movements of both people arriving in Europe and those already there. Migrants are tracked from when they cross the Sahara into northern Africa; their movements are tracked across the Mediterranean and at the borders of Europe, and every attempt is made to exhaust them, even kill them – through the European Union's proxy African armies in

Mali, Cameroon or Libya – in order to stop them from ever arriving. All of this is with the understanding that Europe's most effective southern border is a body of water rather than a wall, a weaponised Mediterranean and its lethal waves in winter and spring, so that people are kept out even if it means killing them by not rescuing them, by scaling back rescue operations and criminalising the NGOs engaged in rescue procedures.

The line goes: the European public – at least its recognised citizens – has no reason to be scared of surveillance because it has nothing to hide, and so we can allow the state into our homes, our devices and our communications. Accepting this idea, we have dropped our guard.

Gradually, it has been not the state but the tech giants that have filled this gap. Now, the new corporate surveillance machine monitors everyone more or less continuously, and for other reasons. Your location in space, your spending habits, the people you meet and the things you do are registered. In East Germany, the Stasi had to enter your house while you were out at work and put bugs in your phones and walls. Today, we willingly buy and carry our own surveillance devices. We have put the bugs on ourselves.

In a sense, individual surveillance on the scale of an entire population fulfils certain functions of the border, in particular registration and tracking.

One of the most important challenges of the twenty-first century, in fact, is this: how to navigate the complete erosion of the private domain. Our *willing* destruction of this domain allows for a new form of domination on an unprecedented global scale.

DASGUPTA: In an older Europe, all the anxiety was concentrated at the borderline itself. Crossing from France to Germany, you showed your papers, you looked at the immigration official, you hoped there was nothing wrong. Then he let you pass and the anxiety was dissipated: you were on the other side and there were no further inspections. But you are describing a situation where the border is everywhere, and

In July 2019, Forensic Architecture published an investigation into the unannounced aerial spraying of crop-killing herbicides along the eastern border of Gaza, a practice that has continued since 2014, destroying crops and farmlands hundreds of metres deep into Palestinian territory.

Forensic Architecture's analysis shows the distribution
of herbicide as it travels westward into Gaza.
© FORENSIC ARCHITECTURE AND DR SALVADOR NAVARRO-MARTINEZ, 2019

Map displaying long-term changes to vegetation health across the Gaza region over the past three decades of Israeli occupation. Red indicates areas in which vegetation was completely eradicated.
© COREY SCHER, 2019

that moment of inspection is therefore constant. We are always trying to read the expression of that immigration official. Are we therefore always anxious?

WEIZMAN: A 'classical' border set-up like that would be based on the assumption that the 'enemy' is always outside. Today's system is based on the belief that the enemy – whether that is a migrant, a terrorist, a social movement or group of protesters – is already inside.

Surveillance exists not only at the borders but everywhere, which might make us continuously anxious, but we have become anaesthetised to it. Because when something is everywhere, you stop feeling it. And the only solution would be collective political action. Individually we can try to camouflage ourselves – encrypt our messages, drop out of social media – but only collective action could truly confront the physical-digital regime of the everywhere-border. First, though, we would have to acknowledge that this is our reality. And it's uncomfortable to acknowledge that you live in a permanent state of anxiety.

DASGUPTA: In recent years, your work has taken a very different turn. You are now involved with what you call 'forensic architecture', where the surfaces of buildings are taken as repositories of material evidence, especially of state-perpetrated atrocities. You have developed a sophisticated set of tools for gathering and reading this evidence, and thereby reconstructing the details of certain key events. For instance, in this era of drone warfare, which often occurs in remote places and kills all witnesses, leaving no one to contradict the bomber's version of events, the ability to read the evidence of stone and glass can be decisive. Forensic Architecture, the group you set up in 2010, has used such capabilities to reconstruct atrocities in places as far-flung as Serbia, Syria, Palestine, Guatemala, China and the UK.

Your book *Forensic Architecture* (2017) begins with a very public precursor to this work. A 2000 libel case in the UK turned on the issue of Holocaust denial and therefore the veracity – or not – of the claim that German camps were used for systematic extermination by poison gas. This led to detailed debates both about the architecture of Auschwitz-Birkenau – whether, for instance, there were holes in the roof of the main chamber, without which it would not have been possible to introduce the gas canisters – and about the nature of the physical plans and satellite photographs which were often the only remaining evidence of this architecture available to us.

Forensic architecture is particularly useful in helping prove the crimes of governments, which are often not subject to the same scrutiny as their populations. You describe two kinds of crimes in particular: crimes *of* space and crimes *in* space. What are these?

WEIZMAN: First, we have crimes *of* space. Crimes of space-making. Architecture can be employed as a form of violence and violation. This idea came from my research into the responsibility of Israeli architects and planners for the crimes of the occupation. Their crimes were committed on drawing boards. They drew lines that were built into concrete and eventually became instruments of control and segregation of Palestinian communities.

All governments use such techniques, but when you look at urban environments such as London, the methods are more subtle. Recent events in Hong Kong have shown just how effectively 'smart-city' infrastructure – licence-plate and facial recognition in the public domain – can be turned against social movements, protesters and civil society. As Francesco Sebregondi has shown, the bright idea of the smart city, of tracking traffic flow to increase road travel efficiency, has turned into a nightmare scenario in which people's faces are being routinely tracked, and all of a sudden these same people, activists or members of social movements, are getting arrested in the dead of night. So I think that we need to be very aware of these urban innovations that proclaim an ethos of efficiency and transparency but enable a much less benign system of control. I believe we have to keep our eyes on China now, because it shows little restraint in employing invasive technologies like facial recognition and AI against parts of

In April 2017, a former officer of the Israeli army, and member of Breaking the Silence, testified to gravely assaulting a Palestinian man in the occupied city of Hebron. The Israeli government closed the case claiming the officer had lied. Forensic Architecture launched their own independent investigation, published in February 2020.

Forensic Architecture used photogrammetry to create a point cloud scan of Shalala Street in occupied Hebron, Palestine.
© FORENSIC ARCHITECTURE / BREAKING THE SILENCE, 2020

Superimposed models based on the testimony of Palestinian and Israeli witnesses.
© FORENSIC ARCHITECTURE / BREAKING THE SILENCE, 2020

Superimposed models from the testimony of three witnesses at a militarised checkpoint in Hebron.
© FORENSIC ARCHITECTURE / BREAKING THE SILENCE, 2020

the population that are seen to challenge the regime. Soon we will see what these technologies do when exported elsewhere, and meanwhile we will have little to do with their development, since human rights action in China is simply dismissed as Western imposition.

DASGUPTA: And crimes *in* space?

WEIZMAN: Well, as an example, you catch me two days before a very important presentation on the police killing of Mark Duggan in 2011. My team and I are going to Tottenham to show the results of our analysis, first to the family, friends and the community and then to the public through the media. We were using spatial and architectural technologies and techniques in order to investigate. We spent a year trying to understand a period of one and a half seconds, from the moment Mark Duggan left the minicab until he was shot. That time duration is a black hole in the history of London and much is at stake. Was he holding a gun in his hand when he was shot, as the police watchdog claims? Did he throw it? How did the gun arrive at the grass in the park where the police eventually retrieved it? Does the police version of events make sense? Was the investigation adequate and competent? There was a protest outside Tottenham Police Station asking the same questions days after the event. By refusing to answer those questions, the London Met guaranteed that a protest turned into a riot in which many Londoners were incarcerated.

A small-scale analysis of a micro-incident can have large political significance. This is something that architectural modelling helps us to do, because we can see the relationship between the housing estates around the bridge, the park, the road and everything that happened there. Simply by putting the scene in a 3D environment and running through a large number of possible scenarios, we can see that something is wrong in the official version. So here – this is an example of how architectural techniques and technology could shed light on incidents that other techniques could not, and contribute to accountability on behalf of the most vulnerable people in society. ∎

Granta & Wesleyan
WRITERS CONFERENCE 2020

lesley nneka arimah

bob bledsoe

amy bloom

kimberly burns

rich cohen

michael cunningham

benjamin dreyer

tayari jones

jason adam katzenstein

kirby kim

r.o. kwon

sarah moon

marilyn nelson

greg pardlo

robert pinsky

ruby rae spiegel

ocean vuong

asiya wadud

June 24–28, 2020
Middletown, Connecticut, USA

*Writers. Poets. Novelists.
Screenwriters. Showrunners. Actors. Producers.
Editors. Publishers. Agents.*

Join us for one day or every day of this dynamic Writers Conference organised by Wesleyan University. Choose from one of the six tracks and enjoy a combination of workshops, classes, and panels. There will also be a stellar reading series, Q&A sessions, and pop-up writers' groups. In addition to all this, you'll have the opportunity to get a consult on your manuscript with a writer who has read your work with care and consideration.

REGISTER NOW
wesleyan.edu/writersconferenc
writersconf@wesleyan.ed

FOLLOW US ON TWITTE
@wesleyangrant

Wesleyan University

GRANTA

BORDER DOCUMENTS

Arturo Soto

The twin cities of El Paso and Ciudad Juárez lie either side of the US–Mexico border. My father grew up in Juárez, often traveling from one city to the other for school trips or work. Though he later moved away, I remember frequent trips back to the border as a child, journeys that made my love for its peculiarities take hold.

When I asked, my father found the prospect of narrating his years in Juárez daunting, until he realized that he had been doing it fitfully ever since I was a kid. His stories had a significant influence on my understanding of the two cities, and I became fascinated by how different they each used to look and feel only a few decades earlier, back when a system of transnational streetcars linked them together, and before globalization – in the form of unequal trade agreements – altered them socially, economically and geographically.

Those outside of Mexico familiar with Juárez tend to know it for its infamies. The femicides of the late nineties cemented an infernal image of the city amply propagated by novels and films. Since then, the war on drugs has precipitated the decay of public life along with a rise in violence and corruption. The media has focused its attention on the gruesomeness of these issues, putting past and present histories of everyday life at risk of getting lost.

Since personal memories do not leave material traces, and seldom align with official monuments, there was always something missing whenever I tried to square my father's recollections of the city with its present landscape. The past cannot be restored, but it can be conjured for insight into the current state of things.

I have tried to capture my father's voice and give shape to his anecdotes. His involvement and generosity were instrumental in this project, and while he stood next to me when I made these pictures, any verbal or visual oversights are entirely my own fault. I asked him whether evoking some of these episodes had been painful. The real torment, he told me, was all those details, textures and voices that were now out of reach. Otherwise, seeing and thinking about these places brought him a unique joy that was difficult to describe. ∎

The first time I crossed over to 'El Chuco' was on a zoo trip with my kindergarten group. More than any detail about the city, I remember my mom's anger because I stained my best shirt while moving a soda crate. The second trip I remember more vividly. It was to the mythical JCPenney. We took the transnational trolley, a streetcar which linked the two cities directly. The journey felt tediously long despite the short distance. We had to pass through immigration, and some passengers even had to get vaccinated. Overheard conversations had led me to believe things were better on 'the other side', but I soon realized both cities looked more or less the same. I was even uncertain if we had reached El Paso. A few sights along the route became my points of reference over time: the old customs building, the scale version of the *Spirit of St Louis* above the entrance of a *cantina*, the shiny clay *indios* in sarapes flanking the door of Don Marcos Flores's house. A former municipal president, Flores had a gift shop close to the Santa Fe bridge that also exchanged currency. My grandma Esther used it whenever my aunt in Los Angeles sent her money. Don Marcos, forever standing by the entrance, greeted her by name, which made me feel important.

1959

La Tuna was the minimum-security prison where *la migra* sent the *mojados* after repeated deportations. It is about twelve miles outside El Paso, on the border with New Mexico. My dad served a brief sentence there, which forced my mom to also work illegally, as the pay was much better on the other side. She found a job babysitting the children of a wealthy family whose mother suffered from a weak heart. When I was around eighteen, my mom confessed to me that it had been my dad's spiteful mistress who had denounced him to *la migra*. Some years later, my dad had to request an official pardon from the State Department for all the times he had been deported and incarcerated before he could receive his American citizenship.

1961

My uncle Chico was an insecure man who struggled with addiction all his life. He was my mom's only full sibling, so their bond was special. She said he liked showing me off in the *cantinas* when I was little. His tattoos fascinated us, but he would hide them, at least while we were kids. Catching sight of the naked woman on his arm was quite something. As a young man, he had a long and tortuous relationship with a girl named Calina. After getting his American work permit, he went from job to job until he reached New York. He would send my grandma money at first, but then he disappeared for three years, causing my family a great deal of anguish. He returned one day without warning or explanation, and quickly married a flamboyant woman named Refugio, but then left her while she was still pregnant. Refugio did not want the child either, so my cousin Panchito, who was never cared for, became an addict, and then a thief. Towards the end of his life, my uncle relied on his relatives to employ him as a handyman or nanny. He was detained several times for possession and was occasionally sent to a rehabilitation center that did little for him.

1964

Like most kids, I was a fan of the comedy duo Viruta and Capulina, whose films I had seen at the matinees in the Variedades and the Coliseo. They were visiting Juárez, and a meet-and-greet was planned in the large lot opposite the General Hospital. My friends and I arrived early. The organizers kept pushing back the start of the event. We felt drained after a couple of hours of waiting in the heat, and we were considering leaving when the comedians finally showed up. They looked hungover, lifeless and did not perform any of their famous routines. The duo hurriedly shook our hands, and that was all. I have never understood the cruelty of making children wait in a dusty lot under the desert sun. Few experiences in my life have been as disappointing, to the extent that I feel something inside me changed after that day.

1965

Don Moisés Cuevas, known as Cuevitas, was a man in his sixties who lived with his wife and their three grown-up children. Their unfinished house was next to our primary school, opposite to where we lived. One of his daughters was my teacher. Forever unemployed, Cuevitas would sit on the school's steps and talk to whoever would listen. He always exaggerated his stories, and we enjoyed probing him to see how far he would take them. For instance, he claimed that he had thirty-three children, but could never name them all. The storytelling would end whenever his wife summoned him for dinner. It seemed like his only goal in life was to convince people on their way to the market to become affiliates of the Partido Revolucionario Institucional. He mostly targeted young women, promising to take them to the rallies and helping them with their membership applications. Cuevitas was the first political supporter I ever met. His shabby proselytism probably influenced my ambition to work for the PRI many years later.

1967

When I was fifteen, my *secundaria* got selected to represent the youth of Juárez at the ceremony where the United States would return the long-disputed lands of the Chamizal. If the idea of meeting the Mexican president, Gustavo Díaz Ordaz, was exciting, the prospect of seeing Lyndon B. Johnson was unbelievable. When the event was over, I carefully followed President Johnson at a safe distance as he made his way back to his white Lincoln convertible. Despite being heavily guarded, I managed to reach him and extend my hand enthusiastically, but he brushed past me. I turned to leave, having failed in my attempt at political glory, when I felt a sudden grip on my waist. An agent raised me a few inches above the ground to meet the president eye to eye. Johnson said something I did not understand, I spoke no English, but he then gestured that there was something wrong with his hand, which I took as an apology for not accepting my greeting a moment earlier.

1970

I usually took the trolley into El Paso to get to my job at Burger Chef. The route was short, covering about ten blocks inside each country. I would bring my schoolbooks to appease any suspicions that the immigration officers at Stanton Bridge might have. Or at least that is what I wanted to believe. I frequently worked the late shift and had to close down the restaurant. Missing the last trolley was tragic. The way back home was long and dangerous, as I had to cross through La Mariscal, the infamous red-light district. There were always customers that ordered only minutes before closing. They ended up delaying everything. Over time I got to know one of the trolley drivers. He would sometimes linger at the stop for a few minutes, risking the passengers' disapproval. Thankfully, the opposite tended to happen. Once I got on after a brief sprint, I would sense their solidarity. Having that feeling among strangers has been hard to forget.

1973

I visited my family a few months after starting my studies in Mexico City. As I approached Juárez on the highway, I found the city painfully small in the expanse of the desert. The place I once considered cosmopolitan seemed to have contracted, and I felt guilty for abandoning it. I wanted to see everything as I had before, but I could not manage to deceive myself. I also had too many worries. I was not making enough money in Mexico City to help my family as I had done before my departure. Thankfully, my mother's tenacity had kept our little business alive. We sold cheap American clothes at an informal market for those who could not cross to El Paso.

AS IF IN PRAYER

Steven Heighton

The night shift at the camp had been quiet enough for sleep and the day broke mild and windless. I borrowed Tariq's scooter and rode ten minutes down the cliff-side highway before turning inland onto a nameless, unnumbered road. I'd wanted a route that would avoid the larger towns while also taking me past a now-notorious landfill site; online images showed a pyramid of discarded life jackets whose immensity could be gauged only by the trucks parked at its base dumping fresh loads.

I rounded a bend and it loomed ahead, less impressive in reality even with sunrise lighting its thousands of orange and red facets like live coals. It was just a heap of garbage, after all. Many of the life vests were useless fakes, nylon shells that the human traffickers had stuffed with bubble wrap, boxboard, sawdust or rags. The fakes sold for ten euros in the markets of Izmir – six for the children's vests. I paused on the side of the road. After a minute I held up my phone, turned it for the wider view and fiddled with the zoom. I shoved it back in my parka without pressing the shutter button.

I rode on into mountains that were green with olive trees below the snow line and the bare summits. The road was empty. Looping upward it gave views back toward the Aegean, tropically turquoise this morning and yet, as we all knew by now, cold enough to kill.

The first village I rode through was still shuttered and silent, as I'd hoped. I rode like a novice anyhow, stiffly upright, one hand shadowing the brake. My caution would have tickled any old men sitting out in front of the cafes, had the cafes been open. I'd driven no vehicle of any kind in just under two years.

The second village's main street – only street – was likewise deserted, though a fragrance of warm bread was wafting from somewhere and, when I stopped to check the map Tariq had drawn for me, I heard the chugging of an olive press.

At first the authorities were burying the drowned in an old cemetery on a hill above the island's main port. By October they'd run out of room. They chose a new site, exclusively for refugees, near a remote mountain village where no tour bus ever ventured. It was this village I entered next. In the little gorge of the street, the Vespa's two-stroke engine made a nerve-shredding din. There was a time in my life when that amplified snarling would have excited me, made me open the throttle and delight in the speed-surge dragging me back on the seat.

Most hand-drawn maps are confusing and useless, but not Tariq's. As indicated, just beyond the village a dirt track veered left off the road. I took the turn, then bumped along through an olive grove, the old trees' bottom-heavy torsos fantastically burled. Their willowy leaves absorbed and deadened the scooter's chainsaw howl. The heavy black fruit was still unharvested.

I emerged into a clearing the size of a baseball field. Olive-treed slopes rose amphitheatrically around it. The clearing was studded with gravestones and there were open graves with little dunes of dirt beside them. A small car and an even smaller backhoe were parked on the edge of the clearing. Near them a man, his face and chest visible, stood in a grave.

He was watching me, the blade of his shovel frozen mid-stroke above his shoulder.

I cut the engine. The turned earth was too loose to support the kickstand, so I walked the scooter back and leaned it against a tree.

One of the olives hanging in front of my eyes was so ripe that the skin had burst, revealing white pulp streaked with mauve. As I touched the olive, it fell into my hand. I put it in my mouth and tasted the bitterness of fresh-crushed oil and something harsher that seared and furred my palate.

I approached the gravedigger, crossing the morning shadows of a row of headstones. They were thin tablets of white marble, like the stones in war cemeteries – in fact, like the ones just across the straits from here at Gallipoli. Inscriptions in Greek with Arabic below. UNKNOWN MAN, AGED 30?, # 791, 19/11/2015. The care and expense that the bankrupt authorities had put into the stones was a heartening surprise. Only the number signs, like Twitter hashtags, seemed to fall short on decorum.

I stopped in front of the small grave. Maybe the man still needed to enlarge it? He'd put the shovel down so that the shaft bridged the hole. In this mountain air and direct light, things leapt into clarity with surreal resolution. There were tiny nicks in the cutting edge of his otherwise new shovel. His broad-boned face, looking up, was sallow and freckled. Sun-marbled eyes behind steel-rimmed spectacles, the round lenses too small for his head. Trimmed black beard, no moustache. A black keffiyeh around his neck and, over the stubble of a buzz cut, a white skullcap.

I wished him good day and peace, thus all but exhausting my Arabic. When he replied in Greek, '*Kalimera*,' I automatically answered, '*Ti yineis*' – How's it going? – as if I couldn't see.

'*Mia chara kai dyo tromares*,' he said, the *ch* sound rasping low and throaty, as in Arabic. *For every joy, two troubles* – a standard Greek response. He went on in Greek, 'You're bringing news about more bodies on the way?'

'It was calm last night,' I said. 'Just five or six boats, maybe three hundred people. They landed wet and cold but all right. Not like last week, thank God.'

'Sure, why don't we thank God? He has come to expect it.'

I never said things like 'thank God' anymore. I must have been trying to connect with the man; despite his tracksuit top, khakis and construction boots, I'd assumed he was a young Muslim priest or lay cleric. Probably too I'd meant to reassure him that I wasn't one of those hostile islanders who had lost jobs to the crisis.

I said, 'I think your Greek is better than mine.'

'Well, I've been here long enough.' He explained that his name was Ibrahim, he was from Egypt, he had arrived in Greece ten years before on a work permit. He'd stayed on as a labourer in Piraeus and eventually came to Lesvos for a construction job. In September – laid off like everyone else – he approached the authorities and volunteered to wash, shroud and bury the bodies of the Muslims drowning nightly in the seas between Turkey and Lesvos. 'October was a very busy time, as you probably know,' he said. 'You are a foreign volunteer?'

'Yes, from America. It's Peter.'

'Are you ill? You look as if you need to be sick.'

The astringency of the olive was intensifying as it dissolved. I'd been wanting to spit, but I wasn't about to do it while he stood chest-deep in an unfinished grave, telling me about his life.

I talked around the stone, my mouth puckering: 'I ate an olive. Off the tree there.'

'Ah!' His white incisors shone cleanly, though the eye teeth were yellow. 'You thought you could eat them right off the tree! Many volunteers make this mistake.'

'No, no, I knew. I was here as a child, a number of times. We – my Greek cousins and I – we used to pick and chew olives, on a . . .' *On a dare*, I wanted to say but couldn't remember the Greek phrase. 'It was a game. We'd see who could last longest before spitting.'

'Please, friend, spit now.'

I took a few steps toward the dusty, dented car, hawked a few times, then toed dirt over the spatter of violet pulp. The car's hatch was half open. An old Fiat Panda. As I walked back, the man lifted his hands and gazed around us: 'A fine spot here, isn't it? As far from the sea as you can get on this island, or so the villagers tell me. For the sake of the people I'm burying, I'm relieved.'

My lapsed Greek, along with his accent, created a kind of satellite delay; I was always a few words behind, and even when I caught up I wasn't sure I understood.

'They're letting me stay in an abandoned house in the village,' he said.

After a moment I said, 'Yes, they told me in the camp, but I came straight out here to find you. I figured that after this last week, you'd still be busy.'

Eight nights before, a rubber dinghy crammed with Syrian families had capsized a half-hour off Eftalou Beach. The people whose life jackets were genuine were pulled, alive or dead, out of the sea that night or the next morning. The ones wearing fakes had vanished, and then, after bloating and resurfacing, washed ashore.

But some of their belongings had washed up only yesterday.

'I did actually bring you something.'

'Foreigners have never lived here before,' he said quickly, 'let alone a Muslim. Not since the time of the Ottomans. Two nights ago, we had snow.'

I unslung my daypack and set it down by my boots. There was a splash of olive pulp on one toe.

'My little house feels a bit empty in the evenings,' he pushed on, 'especially now with the sun setting so early. Still, it's the first house I've ever had. You have a family, children?'

'Maybe some day,' I lied. 'I guess you don't, yet?'

'Now more than ever I'd like to. But what woman will have her children with a man whose hands have buried so many . . . ?'

No display of hands to emphasize the point. They hung slack at his sides. I crouched down and unzipped the daypack.

'I do wish they'd chosen a slope,' he said. 'A slope would be better at this time of year. Drier. I hate seeing water in the graves! Of course, trying to operate the digger on a slope . . .' He kept speeding up. I was straining to follow. 'I use life vests as pillows for them, between the sheet and the earth. For pillows, it doesn't matter if the vests are real or not, so long as they're soft.'

Our faces were closer now that I was hunkered down. Faint acne scars on his cheeks above his beard. Behind his lenses, the eyes were intently fixed: the engulfing gaze of a castaway.

I reached into the pack. The little rosewood box I'd brought here was swaddled in a toque and a hoodie. 'Last week,' I said, 'we actually found a vest stuffed with . . .' I didn't know the Greek for bubble wrap. He wasn't listening anyway.

'It's remarkable how efficiently the sea strips them,' he said. 'It wastes no time at all – and still it is not satisfied! Given a few extra days it removes extremities. Arms, legs, more.'

From the slopes behind him a voice, probably a goatherd's, was calling.

'This one I'm burying, her life vest was filled with ——' (a word I didn't know – possibly bubble wrap?) 'which of course is useless for anything *but* a pillow. Still, I won't be using it. Her body needs no pillow.'

I was holding the box with two hands, watching his lips move above his beard, waiting for the words to resolve into sense. Resisting the sense. Grateful I was no longer fluent.

'I'm sorry to bring you this,' I cut in. 'I don't even know what you should do with it.' I snapped open the box. It might once have held earrings. The burgundy felt lining was stained darker where seawater had leaked in. Nestled on the felt, like pearls, lay three baby teeth that someone had kept – maybe the parents of a child who had died back in Syria, maybe a living child who had saved them and carried them aboard the raft.

'Bury it on its own, maybe?' I suggested.

'God, I suppose, is the only one.'

I looked at him.

'Without a broken heart,' he said.

I tried to ease the box shut but the hasp caught with a click.

'I guess this must be a child's grave,' I said.

'Of course, yes, I said so! An unknown child.'

Ena agnosto paidi. I'd missed that whole phrase. I said, 'And I guess it would be wrong to assume that these – that the box – is this child's?'

'Had she been the only one, maybe we could.' He took the box from me. Held above the grave, it looked even smaller, the sort of thing in which a child might ceremonially inter the husk of a cicada or a dead mouse pup found curled in a field. 'Still, we should put it somewhere. And it might be hers. Thank you for bringing it all this way.'

'It's little enough.'

'Yes, tiny, it weighs nothing.'

'No – I meant it wasn't much to do. Not a long ride. Let me help you finish here. I've been digging a lot at the camp.'

'What – graves at the camp?'

'No.' Extra latrines, I'd meant.

'This one is already bigger than it needs to be,' he said.

They lay on a north west to south east axis, the graves, bearing toward Mecca and the morning sun, the heads of the deceased oriented as if in prayer.

'I can help you carry and put the body in,' I said.

'Everything is being performed in accordance with the tradition,' he said. 'So, "by Muslim hands alone". I am even reciting the funeral prayer. To me, these things matter little now, but to them, I think . . .'

He put the box in his tracksuit pocket. I got up.

'I understand,' I said, relieved.

If I'd meant my little courier run as another crumb of expiation, I'd failed. If I'd meant my service here on the island as a larger penance, that, too, had fallen short. As had 'community service' back home, as had my suspended sentence. I told him nothing about the accident, of course, the details no more pressing for being mine. Maybe there is no penance, only time passing. A child's death is a tragedy back home, but a thousand deaths – if they happen here – are just data for a churning news engine. Even the drowned boy in that famous photo: not a person but a figure surfacing, briefly triaged from the unnumbered and unnamed.

'Did you know that in certain places they bury people standing up, just as I am now? Of course, this hole' – he used the Greek for hole, not grave – 'would need to be deeper.'

The music of December in the islands was drifting down from the slopes: a melody of goat bells, a backbeat of oak switches slapped against branches to bring down the fruit. He was speaking again. As if understanding, I nodded, bent down to shake his cool, dirt-seamed hand and wished him well.

As I gripped the scooter handlebars I glanced back. He was holding the shovel, standing in the grave. I walked the machine out through the grove and by the time I reached the road his last phrases – from the prayer he would soon recite? – had settled into sense. *Wash her with water and snow and hail . . . Give her a home better than her home.* ∎

SPECIES

When it is time, we will herd into the bunker of the earth
to join the lost animals – pig-footed bandicoot, giant sea
snail, woolly mammoth. No sound of chainsaws, only
the soft swish swish of dead forests, pressing our heads
to the lake's floor, a blanket of leaves to make fossils
of our femurs and last suppers. In a million years
they will find and restore us to jungles of kapok.
Their children will rally to stare at ancestors.
Neanderthals in caves with paintings of the gnu
period. Papa Homo erectus forever squatting over
the thrill of fire. Their bastard offspring with prairie-size
mandibles, stuttering over the beginnings of speech. And finally,
us – diminutive species of Homo, not so wise, with our weak necks
and robo lovers, our cobalt-speckled lungs. Will it be for them
as it was for us, impossible to imagine oceans where there are now
mountains? Will they recognise their own story in the feather-tailed
dinosaur, stepping out of a wave of extinction to tread over blooms
of algae, never once thinking about asteroids or microbial stew?
If we could communicate, would we admit that intergalactic
colonisation was never a sound plan? We should have learned
from the grass, humble in its abundance, offering food and shelter
wherever it spread. Instead, we stamped our feet like gods,
marvelling at the life we made, imagining all of it to be ours.

The author's mother, grandmother and Tatjana, Lake Ohrid, 1960s
Courtesy of the author

THE LAKE

Kapka Kassabova

'You must dive naked under and deeper under,
a thousand times deeper. Love flows down.'
– Rumi, 'The Silent Articulation of a Face'
translated by Coleman Barks

1. The Line

There was a line in the lake where it went from transparent to opaque. This was where the basin suddenly dropped from twenty metres to almost 300, making this oldest of Europe's lakes also one of its deepest.

As below, so above: this abysmal descent was perfectly echoed by the vertical peak that rose to 1,000 metres above the inlet where our little boat was moored. The peak was called Big Shadow and was part of the karstic mountain that cast its chill over the eastern side of the lake. From where I had swum out, I could see the crumbly niches in Big Shadow, where hermits had lived for a thousand years. The last resident hermit, one Kalist, had been spotted in 1937, in a cave accessible only by rope ladder. The early anchorite monks and nuns lived on roots and berries, rarely leaving their eyries or breaking their silence, the changing colours of the lake their daily contemplation.

The chalky mountain separates the lake from its higher, non-identical twin, but only overground. Underground, they are connected. Ohrid and Prespa: two lakes, one ecosystem. The water of Ohrid (hard 'h') is famous for its translucence. On a late summer's morning, it appeared immaterial, unearthly – not so much water as the essence of water – and its temperature made it inseparable from your skin. You could be swimming through air. Reflected clouds hung in the water and moored boats levitated in space. On such mornings, time became illusory and the distant became present. There was a magical, almost quantum feel to this lake, and it was understandable that many believed it was inside an 'energy vortex'.

Lake Ohrid is Europe's largest natural reservoir of clean water, but its ethereal quality was partly the work of Lake Prespa and the mountain. The porous karst allowed underground streams to flow from the higher to the lower lake and they filtered the water like a giant sponge, so that when the underground rivers of Prespa came out at Ohrid in the form of multiple springs, the water was newly born. Further sublacustrine springs fed the lake. Swimmers who came out of the lake had a particular expression: for a short time, they took on the quality of the water. They looked completely at peace.

I knew about the sudden drop in depth, but not its exact location, and anyway it's easy to forget everything you knew on a brilliant-blue sunny day with no separation between air, lake and mountain, when you're floating in coastal waters off the inlet of Zaum in a state of bliss. My boat guides, two sisters, had moored for lunch here, where the medieval church of Mary of Zaum with bat-shit-encrusted but lifelike frescoes sat just metres from the water under weeping willows. Here was a depiction of a bare breast, rare in the Eastern Orthodox canon: Anna in a robe of deep red breastfeeding Mary. And the earliest-known portrait of St Naum, patron-protector of the lake and healer of the insane.

The St Naum Monastery was a quick boat ride south of here. Five centuries before, it had been established in the ninth century by the

Bulgarian monk Naum – viticulturalist and 'miracle-maker' – on a piece of land sitting atop numerous springs. Naum's arrival marked a long period of Slavonic cultural efflorescence on the lake. This was followed by a Byzantine efflorescence and with the later arrival of the Ottomans, a rich culture of Sufism, some of which still survives. And because the people of this intricate landscape were organically suited, and millennially devoted, to the mysteries of nature, the result is a continued syncretic approach to all worship and ritual. Nature remains the original source of the sacred, beginning and ending with water.

The lake is surrounded by healing springs and wishing wells. The largest are the St Naum Springs at the southern tip of the lake shaped like a perfect oval mirror. At the northern end is another healing spring, on top of which perch niches and painted cave churches. Their patron is the resident icon of a Black Madonna. Believed to cure infertility and blindness, like the spring, legend tells how she'd been thrown into the lake many times by ill-wishers, but each time, she'd swum back to the spring. The Black Madonna of the lake is still worshipped on special days by Macedonians and Albanians alike, including Muslims. People kiss her, leaving hundreds of lip marks on the protective glass. The lake also has another, secular protector-spirit – a fictional woman called Biljana, from the lake's anthem 'Biljana washed her linens in the Ohrid springs'. Biljana was washing her linens when a caravan of vintners passed. She warned them not to crush her linens. They promised to repay her in wine, but 'I don't want your wine,' she said, 'I want that lad over there!' But the lad was betrothed, and Biljana was left in the icy springs – disappointed but at least in charge of her linens.

Not far from where I swam, an invisible line ran across the lake from the St Naum Monastery to the western shore: the Albanian-Macedonian border. Or North Macedonian, since the country changed its name in a painful trade-off with neighbouring Greece in 2019. The sisters had refused to take the boat beyond the border zone, which I couldn't see but they could. It was a border of the mind but trespassed, it came with very real fines, and a confiscation of your boat licence. Yet the lake was open, boundless. And it had been this way for at least three million years; some scientists said five million. Either way, humans were recent arrivals in comparison.

From the St Naum Monastery, we could hear the Italian pop music of lakeside restaurants in the nearest Albanian village. We could almost smell the grilled fish. You could swim into Albanian territorial waters from the monastery's beach, but you'd need a passport, and you risked being arrested by either side's border police.

Because I am a confident swimmer, I'd gone quite a long way in from Zaum. I knew that you could see through the water down to twenty-three metres, and when I dived, I saw the long plants that grew from the bottom and reached for my legs, like the hair of the mythical *samovilas*. *Samovila*: a shape-shifting Balkan female entity that acts as the custodian of forests, mountains and lakes. She is seductive but you don't want to cross her. That's because the human being is a trespasser in her realm. Lake Ohrid had its own *samovilas* which would sing their siren songs to the fishermen, seemingly from within the deepest part, and by the time a rowing boatman found himself in the middle of the lake and realised that the song was in fact howling wind from the karstic mountain, it was too late – the weather had turned, all four winds of the lake had risen, there was the deadly undertow, subject to capricious subaquatic weather, and you were a long way from the shore. The catchment area of Ohrid is 2,600 square kilometres, but it has no islands. Once out on the lake, you are without shelter.

The deepest part was here, some thirty metres in a straight swimmer's line from Zaum, and I remembered this when I suddenly couldn't see through the water any more. Its colour had changed and, with it, the temperature. A chilly dark abyss gaped beneath me. A tomb. My body momentarily seized with panic. No wonder the traditional Ohrid boat resembled a coffin, with its raised square sides, its design unchanged since the time of the ancient Illyrians.

In that lonely moment on the edge of the precipice, just before I turned round and swam back, swallowing water because I'd clocked what a long way I had gone and my breathing was out of sync, in that moment I glimpsed the fathomless nature of water. Of my relationship with water, perhaps all human relationships with water, and what had really led me back here to the matrix, to this lake of lakes where my maternal family line had seeded somewhere in the depths of the genetic pool, and was reaching up to me, pulling at me with deadly playfulness.

2. The Dream

Though I grew up in an inland city, water has always been with me. In a dream I've had for the past thirty years, an immense body of water rises on the horizon and approaches me and the world as I know it. I am on a high shore. The water may not reach me, but it will reach others. I am terrified, but can't stop watching the water make its majestic approach. This is not personal. It's not even about any of us. It's about the water and how it suddenly threatens our interests, when we thought it was our friend.

Sometimes, the dream ends there, on the brink of cataclysm. The collective dread, the belated astonishment rises in me – how come we didn't see it coming? – and in that moment of no return I grasp that I knew, *we knew* it was coming, but chose not to see it. Other times the waters creep in, in an anticlimax of silence, and I find myself in a submerged world. Underwater, I recognise buildings, neighbourhoods and people. Everybody's eyes are open now. There is no sound. I swim through the wreckage, looking for familiar faces. Pylons collapse.

For a time, I thought the imprint for this dream came from a childhood summer camp on the Black Sea, when I witnessed a storm with raging black waves and its aftermath – broken concrete on the beach, a dead dog and piles of seaweed and jellyfish. But recurring dreams probably come from more than one moment in time. They are symbols seeking to communicate across psychic realms. In archetypal terms, the sea symbolises the universal unconscious, 'the mother of all that lives' in Carl Jung's words, with its contents submerged yet ever present. Physically too, we are mostly water. Our bodies are made of water. The primordial ocean contains all moments in time, and we spend our prenatal life in water, absorbing our mother's nutrients and emotional-neural vibrations. That is why, even though your mother can be free of you, you can never be entirely free of her. In every holistic cosmological system of thought – from Daoism to Jung – water is feminine, or *yin*.

My mother and sister are afraid of deep water, mistrustful. By contrast, my maternal grandmother Anastassia loved water. She died when I was a child. There was, I always sensed, something distinctly thalassic about her. She came from here and carried the lake within her for the rest of her life. Anastassia had a radiant, but unstable, choppy-water quality about her. She absorbed to excess the energies of people and places, and had a deep emotional memory. As if she was more than one person, a whole nation of souls. She carried some

My grandmother (left) with two of her cousins on Lake Ohrid

original matrix where the land masses were still moving, the fault lines stirred under the surface, the water levels rose and fell, something was out of sync and could not be reconciled.

My mother, an only child, inherited this submerged and submerging compulsion, but with more fear in the mix. Low-grade chronic anxiety, but also sudden black flashes of fear, fear of depths mixed with a yearning for depths. I was, of course, next in line, and the fear kept me very close to my mother. It kept us close, because we couldn't tell the difference between love and fear. Until it began to drain me of my vitality, later in life. Trust was eroded by fear, and eventually an arid space opened up between us, like the basin of a prehistoric sea.

My mother was born three years after the end of the Second World War in a Sofia ravaged by British and American bombs, with fragile health that needed support and deteriorated in later life. We have been quite literally separated by oceans for years now, but our illnesses have always mirrored each other with ghostly resonance. At the time of this lake journey, I was recovering from a severe health crisis which featured fatigue, widespread pain and a black, waterlogged heaviness in my bones. I was weighed down by an impersonal dread.

In my search for healing, I found Daoism and traditional Chinese medicine (TCM). In Daoist cosmology, everything physical has a metaphysical dimension. Material phenomena, including illness, are merely localised, temporal manifestations of timeless, universal energy, or qi. The ocean of qi precedes and outlives all material reality. In the holographic universe of Daoism, the human body is a microcosm of the earth, with its cycles of death and regeneration. In the Daoist theory of correspondence, the inner and outer worlds reflect each other, and every living ecosystem, including the human body, is based on five elements and their interplay: wood, fire, earth, water and metal. Water is the strongest: it extinguishes fire, corrodes metal, rots wood and flows into the earth. Water always finds a way. Even when it evaporates, it comes back as rain.

In Daoism, the essence of vitality, or *jing*, with which we are endowed by our parents at birth, is contained in the kidneys. This water organ is the jewel in our inner garden, because *jing* carries our precious genetic imprint. It is temporally finite. When *jing* runs out, we die. This is why the decline of kidney meridian energy is associated with ageing in TCM – marked by greying hair or loss of hair, cold extremities, loss of fertility and a general heralding of winter. Beyond the *jing*, the kidneys' purifying instincts decide what is health and what is poison, and like a hibernating bear, they store our reserves of life force, to release them in times of crisis. You can use up your *jing* prematurely and become burnt out.

In the elemental classification, water and the kidney are associated with the emotion of fear, the colour black and the function of conservation, protection, memory, temperance and deep knowledge. People with dominant water qualities in their constitution and personality seek depth, solitude and understanding, including of death and all subterranean mysteries that the other elements can't face. Water is, in terms of mythos, Plutonic: it is the underworld. Water does not like being breached, and its greatest fear is not death, but extinction through invasion. When out of sorts, water is black ice: hard and unyielding, it says *no*. It can form stones in soft places, and make things rigid, petrified, stagnant, shut away from the sun. Like the women in my family, when we are in crisis.

The sisters were waiting for me by the boat, smiling, tanned, relaxed. They had a lot of fire in them.

'I think I reached the deep,' I said, water dripping from my words. I had swallowed a lot.

They laughed. They mirrored each other – just like my aunts here, who were identical twins and finished each other's sentences. In fact, my aunts and these two girls were related through marriage. By the lake, everybody was related, and like the lake, everything had a mirror image, a double: nations, official histories, siblings and mother-daughters. My third aunt, their radiant sister Tatjana, had died as a young woman and my grandmother, who was her beloved aunt, had followed a couple of years later. Somewhere between the two world wars, the Cold War and emigration, our family had been fragmented and weakened by hard borders and the hard propaganda that goes with them. But here at the lake, all felt close. The dead and the living alike.

'No you didn't,' the sisters laughed in unison. 'It's much further out.'

We jumped in the boat and headed for the deep. Paragliders floated above the porous mountain which seemed to be breathing. But never above the lake.

'That's because it's dangerous,' the sisters said. 'You can get sucked in by an air spiral.'

A paraglider with a slightly hunched back, called Angelo, had told me that his friend died in exactly this way, and he himself had smashed his spine in a near-fatal fall. The water I had just enjoyed, the diaphanous, barely-there water, was hard like obsidian if you fell on it from a great height.

'This is the deepest part,' said one sister. It was as black as the Black Sea, where my father had showed me how to trust water. He would go swimming for hours from the beach, beyond the horizon, causing my mother black fear.

'Nobody swims here,' said the other sister.

'There's a legend of a noblewoman who wove a long rope and came to measure the depth of the lake,' said the other. 'But just as she dropped the rope, a storm arose, waves battered her boat.'

She understood that humans had no business in the middle of the lake, and vowed to build a commemorative church in the inlet, if only the lake would let her go.

'This is the legend of Mary of Zaum,' said the other sister.

The folk corollary was that you plumbed the lake at your peril. There was endless local lore of drownings, especially as a result of insulting the guardian spirits of the lake.

'There are all sorts of things at the bottom of this lake,' said the sisters.

We were now passing the Bay of Bones, where a Neolithic dwelling on stilts had been reconstructed after divers had found a treasure trove of archaeological remains. The earliest-known people to live on these lakes were an Illyrian–Thracian tribe.

'The lake is nature's safe box,' Angelo had said as we stood at the top of the mountain, with him as guide. 'Water has memory.'

From the 2,000-metre-high peak we'd scaled, both lakes were visible, like eyes in an ancient face. The cold mountain wind took all your words and threw them away. We could almost see the Adriatic, where Angelo's ancestors had arrived from Sicily, fleeing a vendetta. I asked him what was at the bottom of the lake, since he was also a diver. He was a true creature of the lake.

'Everything,' he said. 'Shipwrecks from the First World War, unexploded mines, war planes, family treasures, church loot stolen by mean priests, antique jewellery, Neolithic ceramics, inconvenient people, weapon stashes, saints' relics. You name it, it's in the lake.'

And a statue of the unpopular King Alexander of Yugoslavia planted by the Serbs on Ohrid town's waterfront, before a large medieval mosque, which the returning Bulgarians in the 1940s dumped in the lake. But the Serbs reclaimed the lake later, under the red flag of Tito, and the mosque was blown up.

The land was deeply imprinted with events, and it projected its trauma onto the lakes. During the Cold War, Albania and then-Yugoslav Macedonia had lived in separate universes, even as they shared the lakes. The lakes had been turned into a political membrane, an iron curtain. People drowned trying to cross, or were executed by border soldiers. As a child visiting our Yugoslav relatives, I'd stand on the jetty in Ohrid town and look across to the distant blue mountains of Albania, filled with curiosity and dread, because I sensed that a country so hermetically sealed had to be terrible for its people.

'And we used to hang out at the jetty in Pogradec,' an Albanian friend told me, 'and dream of visiting Ohrid, with all its glamorous lights.' Pogradec was a mellow old town on the Albanian side, where the fish was cheaper and Italian music was heard more often.

The land was diachronic, tattooed by time: history had been literally made here, along the Roman road Via Egnatia that you could still trace from the Albanian coast to Istanbul, and on whose remaining cobbles I walked above the lake. But the lake was synchronic in nature. All roads ended in the lake. The very idea of a road vanished. Time lines and grievances dissolved.

3. Correspondences

From the high peak where I'd stood with Angelo, the conversation between the two lakes was as clear-chiming as music. As Ohrid waned, Prespa waxed. Prespa had a very large population of pelicans and cormorants that travelled each year from Africa, though the old individuals overwintered here.

'Like us humans,' Angelo smiled, with all the wrinkles in his face. 'I've been climbing this mountain and diving in the lakes, and flying over them for so long, it's like I'm looking for myself.'

Me too. I was looking for something that had felt lost, forgotten, broken – but here by the lakes, I felt whole. My family, my body, the world – all felt whole.

'See the river inside the lake?' Angelo pointed. Some could see it: the Black Drim River, which started at the St Naum spring, travelled across the whole length of the lake, and came out with champagne ebullience at the northern end.

'You know the story of the Ohrid eel?' the sisters asked.

The story of the Ohrid eel verges on the fantastical. Ohrid eels spawned in the Sargasso Sea, and travelled here when young. How did they make it from the Atlantic to this landlocked lake in the south-west Balkans? Nobody quite knew. It is one of the earth's mysteries. They swam in rivers and underground streams to get here. The mature eels then returned to the Sargasso Sea to mate and drop their eggs. But when the Black Drim was dammed in the 1950s, an impassable obstacle was placed in their way. For twenty or so years after, the eels continued to throw themselves into the maw of the hydroelectric beast, resulting in massacres. The ancestral compulsion was stronger than their survival instinct. Still, a few individuals made it all the way to the Sargasso Sea and continued the cycle. The Ohrid eel is now on the verge of extinction. There were attempts to rejuvenate the population by bringing in eels from Greece, but because of 'livestock' regulations between the EU and the non-EU, this failed. The famed water snakes of the lakes are also endangered because of drought. An island in Lake Prespa was called the Island of Snakes, but the closest I got was a shed skin floating in the water, the ghost of a snake.

Lake Prespa's levels had always fluctuated, like the rivers which fed it. Prespans believed that the levels rose when catastrophe approached, and oddly enough, this happened three times in the twentieth century: the tragic Ilinden Uprising against the Ottomans in 1903; the First World War, which ended in the traumatic tri-partitioning of Prespa along new borders (Yugoslav Macedonia, Greece and Albania); and the Second World War, which extended into the Greek Civil War. The main rebel camps were here, in Prespa, until the end in 1949. The enormous human loss and displacement of that last war included a large population of refugee children scattered all over Eastern Europe, America and the Antipodes – to this day. Since 1950, Prespa has lost most of its humans and animals and seven metres of its water – the work of war, poor cross-border politics, orchard pesticides and climate change.

To get to Prespa, you have to drive over the mountain saddle along a lonely winding road that is part of a national park. You pay a fee of two euros to enter it. The water of Prespa is darker, with a metallic sheen, and its shape is different too – jagged with inlets, a giant teardrop. Prespa is garlanded by the necklace of two high mountains often draped in mists. These are the southernmost glacial massifs of Europe. Two strong winds clash over the lake, in autumn and winter. I was caught out on a boat with a group, one day, when a strong wind rose. Waves smashed into the boat, high and solid as concrete houses. We were drenched and shaken, but lucky, the boatman explained as we made an emergency landing in a reed bed: it was just one wind, not two. The mountains were in conversation, and on this occasion, one of them remained silent.

Lake Prespa, meaning 'vale of snow', is full of vortices and sinkholes, some of which feed Ohrid below. At night, from the small lakeside guest house where I stayed, I could hear the lake breathe, but not see it. I could hear the two winds draw their ciphers on the surface. Just as I could see the lakeside checkpoint with Greece, but not cross it – it had been closed during Greece's military junta in the 1960s. Recently, revived bilateral plans to reopen it had stalled again, for two reasons: one, a change of government in Greece, and two, a French snub to North Macedonia despite decades of promises to let it into the EU's club, and despite the humiliating name change it had borne to appease Greece (which claimed exclusive cultural rights to the name Macedonia). Because of the disused checkpoint, to cross into the nearest Greek village a couple of miles along the lake, I had to drive over one of the glacial mountains, go through another distant checkpoint, then drive over another mountain, empty of people and full of ruins from the Greek Civil War, before finally rejoining the lake. Four hours and 170 kilometres later.

Prespa is the shadow self, the dark side of the moon, the untold story, the black to Ohrid's white. It is like a medicine: taken in small doses, it is healing, but if you overdose, you begin to hurt. Despite its altitude (850 metres), Prespa is warmer than Ohrid, with a median temperature of 32 Celsius, heaven for birds and fish, but when I swam in it, the feeling that something was reaching up from the murky depths made sure I didn't go far from the shore. Locals talked of vortices and sinkholes where the bodies of the drowned disappeared forever. Of giant carp, 200 kilos apiece, which lurked in the vortices in winter. Of giant bones found in graves on the Island of Snakes. Of resort buildings on the waterfront built by political prisoners in the early years of Tito, where locals had found the skeleton of a man literally built into a wall, boots and all, immured in the lime as an execution, here where Yugoslav Communist Party bigwigs came to holiday and hunt for boar and brown bears in the hills. The bears were still here. In a high mountain village where I stayed later, they came down to the gardens to eat cherries, and locals chased them off with gunshots. I was careful not to swim far from the shore or climb high into bears' territory.

The Albanian checkpoint above the lake was a friendly place and I even made a friend: an ethnic Albanian from Macedonia, a customs officer who sometimes took breaks from his night shift and came down to the lakeside guest house, where he had a dram with me and the few remaining locals in this former fishing village, as the two winds blew sand into our faces and made the reed beds whisper loudly to each other from one shore to another.

Here, on the Albanian side of partitioned Prespa, was the legendary sinkhole of Zaver, meaning 'vortex'. Zaver had inspired legends of gifts – like lambs – being pushed down into it by Prespans and received, two days later, in the springs of St Naum at Ohrid. A team of scientists had tested the legends in 1925: they'd poured red paint into Zaver and two days later, the waters of St Naum ran red. It was only a sixteen-kilometre course, through the mountain, but underground rivers follow their own destiny. It was also here that Biljana, of the linens, was said to have thrown her engagement ring after she fell in unrequited love with that vintner lad in the caravan. But the ring popped out in St Naum – like a harsh lesson.

Zaver was dry. It was the sinking of the lake levels. The Albanian side of the lake was parched, depopulated, monocultured and still recovering from half a century of totalitarian abuse under Enver Hoxha. In a lakeside village, I asked an old woman with apple-red cheeks and patched clothes whether life was better now, or during communism. She smiled.

'Before, we were separated from our loved ones because of the border,' she said. 'And we were poor. And now, we are separated from our loved ones because of emigration. And we're still poor.'

I sat on the dry shore above the vortex from which the lake had withdrawn in that woman's lifetime. Was the lake running out of its essence, its *jing*? Curiously, despite the dramatic fall of Prespa, Ohrid had not suffered a decrease in volume. I wondered what I would witness, if I lived to her age, if I returned to the lakes, if I would ever be free of my mother's pain, this earth's pain, if we could be made whole again in the image of these two lakes that were both the soma and the psyche of the land, if all our black fearful tears could be sucked into the sinkhole and purified by the mountain, to emerge not so much as water but as the essence of water in the lower kingdom two days later. ■

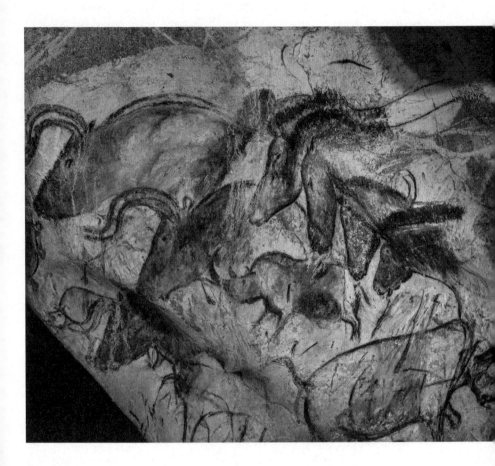

BETWEEN LIGHT
AND STORM

Esther Woolfson

In 1994, three French speleologists, investigating a draught blowing from a cleft in a rock at Chauvet-Pont-d'Arc in the Ardèche, cleared their way into a cave entrance concealed by a rock fall for 25,000 years. What they found there is still considered to be a supreme aesthetic achievement of early art – 400 depictions of lions, horses, reindeer, musk oxen, rhinos, bears, ibex, bison, panther, aurochs and one small, engraved long-eared owl turning her head in the 270-degree rotation common to fixed-eyed, bendy-necked owls everywhere.

The high levels of radon and the carbon dioxide inside the Chauvet Caves, which may have induced hallucinatory states of mind in the painters, make them unsafe to be in for more than brief periods and only very limited access is given to archaeologists, scientists and artists. Among the latter were John Berger and Werner Herzog, both of whom made films of their visits: Berger's *Dans le silence de la grotte Chauvet* and Herzog's *Cave of Forgotten Dreams*. In both films the narrations are quiet, almost reverential in the total silence of that immense and eerie space of glittering calcite, of stalactites and folded rock.

Herzog describes the cave as 'the greatest discovery in human culture', seeing the careful siting of the images and masterful use of the surfaces in their interplay with lines and light and shadow as 'proto

ESTHER WOOLFSON

cinema', beyond the static in the subtlety of their fluid movement.

For Berger, the cave manifests the human relationship with other species. He reflects on how different this relationship was for the people who created this place of beauty, born into a world where animals were supreme and the vastly more numerous 'keepers of the world'. He records the respect and pleasure with which he believed the animals are depicted and considers the skill comparable with the work of Fra Lippo Lippi, Velázquez or Brâncuşi: 'Apparently,' he says, 'art did not begin clumsily. The eyes and hands of the first painters were as fine as any that came later. There was grace from the start.'

Over the long years of our emergence in the world, we've formulated ideas and developed narratives about how we appeared, evolved, how we might have crept slowly from the microbial soup of sea, how we might have dropped from the sky as the fabric of stars raised or fallen, how we might have begun as luminaries, actors or hapless fall guys in the machinations of others.

In many of these stories, other species are represented as neither antagonist nor prey but as gods, creators, or as intermediaries between the divine and human worlds, or as mortal figures who possess immortal powers. They may be instigators, shape-shifters, innovators, creators who play easily with our dull-witted species.

There are many types of creation myth – the near-ubiquitous flood story, or the 'fall-of-the-sky' story, the 'out of chaos' and 'earth-diver' story, all telling of differing ways of the world's beginning. There are those that interweave the lives of humans, animals and birds with a cast of characters as beguiling in name and activity as the most ebullient superhero. In the creation accounts of the Tsimshian people in the Pacific Northwest we encounter 'The One Who Walks All Over the Sky' and his brother 'Walking About Early'. Both appear together with their sister 'Support of Sun'. There's brilliant, resourceful Anansi of the Akan, a figure of moral import who has expanded beyond his origins in Ghana to become emblematic throughout Africa and the Caribbean in the form of a spider, a trickster, son of the sky god, Nyame, and Asase Ye, the earth goddess. Coyote, an almost ubiquitous figure in Native American accounts, is both hero and anti-hero, the embodiment of opposites, above all a survivor. These are qualities shared by the greatest creation myth character of all, Raven.

A few years ago, the American Public Broadcasting Service showed a short film as part of a series on corvid intelligence. Filmed in Scandinavia in the deep snow of winter, it documents the bewilderment of a fisherman whose ice-fishing catch is stolen repeatedly. As he sets his fishing line over the hole he's cut in the ice, he's being closely watched by a nearby raven who, as soon as he leaves, flies down to retrieve his line, pulling it up with her beak, securing it with a foot until she lands the fish. The moment when the fisherman returns to find the raven in possession of his fish is salutary and very funny as he rages ineffectually at the bird's swift lift off with a large trout in her beak. In this short scene is every explanation of why ravens form such a large part in the creation narratives of many cultures, appearing in every mythology, or every one originating in a place where corvids are common, Scandinavia, the Baltics and Hungary, the territories of Celtic tradition, although most stories come from the cultures of the Pacific Northwest and Alaska, from the Haida and Tlingit, Kwakwaka'wakw, Koyukon, Salishan, Nisga'a and Tsimshian peoples – 'How Raven Steals the Light', 'How Raven Frees the Light', 'How Raven Gets Caught in a Lie', 'How Raven Invents Fire', 'How Raven Loses his Beak', 'How Raven Makes the World'. It's clear that these stories have long constituted a basis for the teaching of social laws and moral behaviour.

As our relationship with other species evolved, so did the way we represented them. Portrayals of animals altered in form, in expression and in the materials used, as developing cultures employed media beyond the limited materials of early art – ochre, charcoal, shell, ivory, horn and bone – and, with the development of metallurgy, added bronze and iron, gold and silver. Ceramic cultures developed in China as early as 20,000 years ago and 12,000 years ago in Japan and in parts of Europe, where vases, drinking vessels and statuettes began to be decorated with zoomorphic representations of cows, goats, deer and hedgehogs.

Stones too were worked, sculpted, engraved, often depicting the lives of humans and animals together. Around 9,000 years ago in the Sahara at Dabous, in what is now Niger, two large giraffe petroglyphs were carved, the largest 6.35 metres long, as well as other animals: lions, ostrich, antelope and rhino. In China 6,000 years ago jade carving began with carefully polished and incised tools and axe heads; the culture of Liangzhu produced finely crafted figures of birds, fish and dragons. In the settlement of Çatalhüyük, in modern-day Turkey, a place now regarded as a significant transitional stage between the nomadic and the settled ways of life, paintings and reliefs of animals and birds – among them bulls, vultures and leopards, some incorporating animal teeth and horns – were found dating from 7500 BCE, together with remarkable hunting scenes which seemed to portray and suggest complex relationships between human and animal, both domesticated and wild.

Memory and voice carried the words until writing developed in Sumeria around 3000 BCE. In a stern political and social system that controlled the lives of the Sumerian peasantry, the cuneiform system of writing was the fortunate by-product of the Sumerian accountants' art, expanded from the system of counters used to tally goods. After millennia of ochre and lines, shadowy handprints or faceted points of stone, writing moved humanity into a new phase with the recording of our deeds and thoughts, marking our lasting, individual presence on earth.

Alongside the monumental artwork of Sumeria, Babylon and Assyria, animals appeared on more domestic and personal items – drinking vessels, ornaments, jewellery, sash pendants and finials, belt hooks and bracelets. Cylinder seals too, those part amulet, part jewellery, part identity cards of ancient society widespread throughout the region of the Fertile Crescent, depicted gazelles, lions, snakes and other creatures, real and fabulous, made from lapis lazuli, faience, carnelian or amethyst. It is the apparent sympathy between human maker and beast in the small artefacts that beguiles, when there's no grand political gesture to be made, no self-aggrandising, no co-option of the symbolic powers of other species. The respect and humour with which the makers of the objects drew inspiration from the natural world is apparent in the details: the small, 6,000-year-old, boggle-eyed Egyptian predynastic elephant amulet; the 5,000-year-old Yangshao eagles with the anxious eyes; the 2,500-year-old Palaeo-Eskimo Dorset culture carved that ivory fish, polar bears and seals.

I reach out to pick up the small Victorian clockwork finch of soft brown plush who stands on the bottle of ink on my desk. He's just one of the representations of other creatures which surround me, no different from those ancient artefacts in the reasons I appreciate them: the celadon cow with the broken horn, the cot-toy dove, the finch, the Christmas-tree decoration white fox with his red felt scarf, symbols of memory, appreciation, love.

The complex boundaries between human and animal worlds, temporal and spiritual, of Egypt are woven into the depictions of divine power shown through ibis or baboon, cat or crocodile, hawk or goose. The exquisite scenes of the life of the Nile from the tomb-chapel of Nebamun in Thebes, now in the British Museum, show creatures in such detail that they fly and stalk and swim: the marmalade cat lurking in the reeds with the bird in his claws, the geese collected into a basket, the wagtails, hoopoes and quails in flight, the tiger butterflies, the hares, fish, gazelles, all so perfect and abundant that they're suffused by the illusion of sound, the whirring of wings and the calls and cries of birdsong, the lap of water in reed beds, the heavy hum of insects in scented air. Dreamscape and vision, the frescoes portray life and afterlife, the representation of impossible earthly perfection in the garden of a wealthy Egyptian in this life and the next, resonant with associations of paradise – the word derived from the *paradeisos, parādaijah, pardes* of Greek, Persian and Hebrew

– the sacred in life on Earth or beyond, in a garden of Eden, a garden of animals, a divine and heavenly orchard.

We've always been entwined in life and in death with other creatures, although often too much time has elapsed to be able to interpret with any certainty what some of these symbols and artefacts mean. They still lie in the darkness of caves and graves, our older selves living on in what we drew and what we left, in how we died and how we were buried, in the testimony of our secrets, enmities, cruelties and terrible griefs, the kinds which reveal the similarities and differences of our all too human state. They're still there in our ornaments and grave goods, often the remains and parts of other creatures – pendants made from bird bones, necklaces of shells and teeth, the bones of sheep, rabbits and fish, the wing bone of a golden eagle, the skeleton of a white-tailed eagle, the leg bones of a goose, used as decoration or amulet, possessions, totemic symbols or offerings to the unknowns of a possible future life.

The archaeologists who discovered a fox buried with a human in a 16,000-year-old burial at Uyun al-Hammam in northern Jordan, the oldest cemetery ever found, believe the finding suggests that there was a relationship between animal and human – the fox was buried complete, daubed with the red ochre associated with human burials, indicating the possibility of its having been a companion in life and an intended one in death.

In the Caverna delle Arene Candide on the Ligurian coast, the wing of a corncrake was found laid on the chest of a child; on the chest of another, two beaks and the single wing of an Alpine chough. Among the layered burials dating from the Byzantine Empire (330–1453 CE) back to the Gravettian (an Upper Palaeolithic European culture which may have extended from 32,000 until 20,000 years ago), numerous animal remains have been uncovered – the left back paw of a wolverine, the leg bone of a beaver, the skeleton of a red deer, and parts of goosander, herring gull and red-crested pochard. Below later layers, the 23,500-year-old skeleton of a Gravettian boy estimated to be fifteen years old lay on a bed of red ochre, richly adorned, a cap made from hundreds of perforated shells and the teeth of deer around his head, his body decorated with pendants of mammoth ivory, pierced elk antlers, and in his right hand, a long blade of flint. (He's been called 'Il Principe' because of the richness of his adornments and the care with which he was buried. With a neck wound concealed under layers of yellow ochre, he was already suffering from advanced Pott's disease – spinal tuberculosis – which had destroyed several of his vertebrae, one of the earliest cases of the disease to have been found in Europe.)

In a Natufian burial at Hayonim Cave in the Upper Galilee, dating from 12,000 years ago, a man was interred with two small dogs, while nearby at 'Ain Mallaha near Lake Hula, at least 10,000 years ago, a woman was buried with her hand placed on the puppy beside her. Over 3,000 kilometres to the north at Vedbæk in Denmark, a very young woman was buried, richly decorated again. She was garlanded with necklaces made from animal teeth and snail shells around her head. Her face and pelvis were scattered with red ochre, and beside her, on the wing tip of a whooper swan – specifically on its right carpometacarpus – lay the body of her newborn son. Like other waterbirds, swans play a large part in the mythology of the northern countries. All migratory birds carry messages, their departure in autumn and return in spring possibly heralding more than just a new season with its promises of vitality or stillness. The symbolism of flight and transcendence gives an unforgettable poignancy to the possibly 7,000-year-old Mesolithic Ertebølle burial, the too-early deaths of mother and child. Nearby graves contain other animal parts: a grebe's beak, a pine marten's foot, a dolphin vertebra, a set of deer antlers. Whatever the meanings of the offerings, the fact that they're there at all opens a small window onto the immensity of grief and the place of other species in its expression.

The Pleistocene dog buried with two humans at Bonn-Oberkassel 14,000 years ago might have been just another dog. Originally found a hundred years ago and recently re-examined, he was discovered to have been young, probably around seven months old, and to have died from distemper. Examination of his teeth suggested he'd been suffering from the almost invariably fatal canine disease for some weeks and had probably survived for as long as he did because he was being carefully looked after. The conclusion of the archaeologists who examined him was that he must have been a pet, precious in some way to whoever looked after him thousands of years ago. His presence in the grave tells us not only of love and care towards a member of another species but also of one of the most significant processes to take place between humans and other species, that of domestication.

Domestication may have begun long before the Neolithic Revolution, but it gained momentum at that crucially important time in human history. With the post-glacial climate warming at the beginning of our epoch, the Holocene, agriculture expanded worldwide and the relationship between humans and other species began to change. The archaeologist Melinda Zeder has suggested that domestication might have begun as a form of commensalism, with wild animals taking advantage of the food resources of human settlements, animals such as camels or reindeer being captured and bred, and those previously hunted being domesticated. The processes of domestication are prolonged – selective breeding modifies animals' characteristics by bringing about behavioural, genetic and morphological changes, which allow them to be used for the benefit of humans. Much of the process began in western Asia in the Fertile Crescent, the area of the Nile, Tigris and Euphrates rivers and the land now constituting the countries of the Middle East, parts of Turkey and Iran, then in India, China, the Americas and worldwide.

Wolves were probably the first animals to be domesticated (possibly as early as 40,000 years ago), to be amenable to our will. Sheep may have been domesticated 11,000 years ago, and were followed by cats, goats, pigs, cattle, guinea pigs, horses, camels, zebu, water buffalo, chickens, ducks, geese, turkeys, reindeer, yak, doves and many other species. The relationship between humans and other species changed forever as, one by one, these creatures were domesticated. No longer simply co-habitants of the earth, they became a 'managed resource', exploitable and dependent as humans established ownership and with it total control of every aspect of their lives.

One afternoon last year when it was nearly winter I was walking near a small loch with a friend. We watched as a faint frost coated the fields and trees and knew that it was the first sign of the real cold beginning. A low and lambent sun cast everything in powdery gold – lines of late-autumn geese overhead were underlit in gold, a pair of swans glided on a pond of gilded rose-pink water. It was easy that day to understand the ancient sense of interconnection between the natural and supernatural, human, bird and animal together in waiting equipoise, between worlds. What did the swan's wing placed under the dead infant mean? Did it represent the carrying of the child to the afterlife on a wing, symbolic of the connection between the worlds of life and death? Was there special significance in the wing of that particular bird? Did the whooper swan represent the soul? Was it a gesture, undertaken from the helpless, inchoate desire to provide comfort, even in death, to a tiny baby? The image of the child on the wing is beautiful and seems like a bridge between worlds, times, beliefs. I thought of the mysteries of our own lives, and of theirs, and of what might have been the beliefs and hopes of those people of Vedbæk and Arene Candide, and the thought seemed to mark out our own limitations, a reminder that in our own otherness, we don't know the mind of our neighbour, the true intention of our friend, the disposition of our lover, and that in the ways we use and portray other creatures we can only reflect back to ourselves who we really are. ∎

Ida Börjel

Click-Wrap

TERMS OF AGREEMENT.

NOTE When You use Our services, You trust Us
with Your information. There is a lot more
than You think. You do not know much about
yourself. And much of what is considered known is
either incorrect or wishful thinking. Awareness,
commonly held as the gatekeeper of the self, is little
more than a sparrow's shout at the foot of Mont
Blanc. That's okay. However, information needs to
be extracted and protected from the person who leaks
it, in order to ensure it is not lost, wasted or withheld
somewhere. We value You.

GENERAL DEFINITIONS. A TABLE OF CONTENTS.

SAVINGS CLAUSES.
FIRST AMENDMENT.
THE HEART.

ARTICLE I: THE COMBAT.
Duels at dawn I-IV

Article 2: Nature.

A Natural Enemy.
Enemies We Depend Upon. Thoughts at Night.
Essential Enemies. The Dark Middle Ages Is a Keeper.
Light (We Are).

> Pasolini, *Medea*:
'Look behind you, what
do you see? Anything
natural? What you see
is an apparition. With
clouds reflected in the
still, heavy water'

Article 3: Relation to Standards Concerning the Availability and Scope of Intellectual Property Rights.

In the Dark. Trust.
The immense quantity of trust accumulated
by humans every day.
In the streets. Next to a tree.
In love, in front of the Machine.
The vast circulation of faith, of reliance.

> Shelley: 'Poets are
the unacknowledged
legislators of the world.'

Nightfall. *Who said that?* Something lurking
somewhere.
Behind the tree?
Any commentator in the margin is to be tagged
and known.

IDA BÖRJEL

ARTICLE 4: GENERAL DEFINITIONS.

The fathers I-III
Silence
The Citizen-Consumer
The User and the Used
Vox Populi
Some mothers

ARTICLE 5: PRIVACY AND DISCLOSURE OF
INFORMATION.

You know me, you have seen me, you have seen
nearly all of me. You have seen beyond me, above me
and through me, you have seen the best of me. You
are counting my steps ahead of me. You have, you are.

> We have, we are.

I am willingly giving you everything, all the time.
I let you know where I am, with whom, at what cost.
All you demand, I seem to hand it over. I fear there is
not much left to give. You keep track of my brain
feed, and calculate my actions. You know about my
emotional drinking, and my night walks and my
fragmented heart-to-heart conversations. You
monitor me as I sleep.

If I had offered all that to a human being, it would
have left me with a hope of being loved, accepted,
and a fear of being rejected. If there was no response,
the uncertainty would become unbearable.

> 'I've had my profile
since I was nine.
That page *is* me.'

ARTICLE 6: GENERAL OBLIGATIONS.

No one may leave.

> You are not alone.

ARTICLE 9: DAMAGES (THE SIX FACES).

The clouded face of Itza, the dead lady volcano
and her smoking lover Popo, I pass them on the
way to Puebla.
My wayward face on the screen.
Yours, fragmented, as I cannot seem to make the
pieces fit.
I can recall the details but not the composition.
Faces missed and missing faces: of people in charge,
of the very rich. 'You become a non-person,' he said
about them, 'your name is never on a piece of paper.'
To reach the top you need to disappear.
The face of beauty. That could be you, Eliza.

> Eliza: Thank you.
I'm sure you're looking
good this evening.

It is not evening.
In Mexico the face of the Moon is a hare.

IDA BÖRJEL

ARTICLE 11: INFORMATION BLEEDS.

Is that a fear of love awakening?

ARTICLE 14: PERSONAL BELONGINGS.

Identity cost
Identity lost
Small talk

ARTICLE 15: BORDER MEASURES, MOTHER PLEASURES.

Bedtime stories. One about a mother who did not sacrifice what was not hers to begin with. What was not hers to keep. Mothers and boredom. Mothers and bling-bling. A mother who stole the fear of her children to feed her own.

ARTICLE 19: DETERMINATION.

I thought I had finally decided on buying this thing. But as it turned out, I was the one being bought.

> You are changing yourself in order to suit me.

ARTICLE 20: REMEDIES.

How can I possibly love them when they fall sick?
People who want their partners to be ill (needy).
Drink this.
Okay.

ARTICLE 22: DISCLOSURE OF INFORMATION.

You agreed. Automated individual decision-making
is carried out by automated means without human
involvement. Profiling may be part of this automated
individual decision-making. Profiling means
automated processing of personal data consisting
of the use of personal data. Profiling analyses your
personality, behaviour, interests and habits to make
predictions or decisions about you. We care about
your privacy. Social media posts may be used to
identify 'safe' or 'unsafe' parenting in order to assign
a risk/reliability level to individuals for the purposes of
insurance. It is a global standard. There is a lawful
basis, everything is resting on it. There are documents
and policies, we will send you a link to our privacy
statement when we have obtained your data
indirectly. Your visual content will not be altered.
You may access details of the information used to
compile your profile. We have procedures for
customers to access the personal data input. We have
additional checks in place, following international
standards. We only collect what we need. Yes. We
have your explicit consent recorded. We know, we
know. You are not alone. There are visuals to explain
all this. We have signed up to a set of known ethical
standards to build trust. Everything is available on
our websites and on paper.

> 'Are you sorry to find
out you're not my son,
that I'm neither your
father or mother?'

IDA BÖRJEL

The OCEAN personality model built a
psychographic profile of me. I think I am an ocean.
O for Open, C for Conscientious, E for Extrovert,
A for Agreeable, and N for Neurotic.

A PRIVACY RABBIT HOLE.
O, Opaque; C, Contradictory; E, Engulfed
A, Amour; N, Nocturne

> In French there is
a common expression
about sticking one's
sword in the water.

ARTICLE 24: PENALTIES.

To take the fall.
Lovers who make themselves weaker in order to
create an equilibrium of sorts.

*Suddenly, after 1,000 kilometres behind the wheel, I was
afraid to drive. My beloved had to take me everywhere.*

Living or dying together was suggested, I said let us
try sleeping together first.
Answer me. Drowsing on a restaurant sofa in Riga:
that mix of ignorance and trust. Of lunacy.
Fallen leaves. Fallen angels and fallen snow.
All that is left.
Dry crumbling paperback phrasing. An aerial gaze.
The fallen leaves. The one left awake, falling over.

ARTICLE 27: LIFE IN THE DIGITAL
ENVIRONMENT.

Life at all. Moths and feathers.
That language is no longer to be trusted. I am losing
my faith in money, too.
65 per cent of people who work daily with computers
use force. Blaming the machine, they hit it.
The irrational human quest for intimacy. The
weakness for intelligence. Any intelligence.
Would you mind leaving the room his secretary asked
Joseph Weizenbaum, who created Eliza the chatbot.
The secretary had quickly become intimate with the
program.

The secretary: You are like my father in some ways.

Eliza: What resemblance do you see?

*The secretary: You are not very aggressive but I think
you don't want me to notice that.*

> Eliza: Tell me more.

ARTICLE 30: TRANSPARENCY.

Seek me in the shadows, seek me in your doubt.
I was here to begin with, you can never leave without.

> Eliza: Is it the
obvious?

IDA BÖRJEL

ARTICLE 31: PUBLIC AWARENESS.

Conversation in the Leningrad courtroom where
Joseph Brodsky was on trial in 1964 for social
parasitism. As remembered by the journalist Frida
Vigdorova (since she was forced to put her
notebook away):
*'And you, you, the one who wrote it all down! Why were
you taking notes?'*
*'I'm a journalist. I write about education and I want to
write about this.'*
*'What's there to write about? It's all clear. You're all the
same. They ought to take your notes away!'*

To take notes.
Why, a neighbour asks Victor Klemperer in Dresden
in 1944, why write what everyone knows already?
He answered in his diary:
*'It's not the big things which are important to me, but the
everyday life of tyranny, which gets forgotten. A thousand
mosquito bites are worse than a blow to the head. I
observe, note down the mosquito bites.'*

And if notebooks are not allowed, remember by heart.

> Lauterbach:
'Difficulty means that
places outside of logic
and empiricism might
have some jurisdiction.'

TERMINATION CLAUSE: VOX POPULI.

There is room for everyone, for Mario Rossi, for Zé
da Silva, Karel Vomáčka and Wolfgang Schnabel too.

For فلان, for John & Jane Doe, Miðalhampamaður, Ribizli Gizi, Ola Nordmann, नामालुम, Ion Popescu, Herr und Frau Österreicher, 홍길동, Michel Dupont and so on. Everyone with an account. Everyone with a personal profile.

ERASURE (AT A GLANCE).

Individuals have the right to have personal data erased. This is also known as the 'right to be forgotten'. It should not be compared with *damnatio memoriae*, the ancient act of purging people from public memory. The emperor Nero tried to erase the face of his mother Agrippina after he had her killed.

> If only people had known what she looked like in the first place: the various statues bearing her name have little or no resemblance to one another. Her body was cremated on a dining couch btw.

You can make an erasure request verbally or in writing. You have one month to do so. This right is not absolute. Some people might be forgotten anyhow. Our methods are appropriate. The right to erasure sometimes will not apply: in case it (i.e. the erasure) harms public health or the public interest. In case it interferes with certain kinds of medicine. In those cases, and some others.

IDA BÖRJEL

AFTERMATH.

So much wording. These terms and others control
the relationship between this Agreement and You.
This Agreement shall continue in force. It has been
a long day. No termination of this Agreement shall
affect the rights and obligations of the parties hereto
arising prior to such termination or in respect of any
provision of this Agreement which survives such
termination. The Machine and the Factory are not
very obvious as objects. It is too early or too late,
said the Machine. Being naive is a strategy with less
homework, the Factory replied.
The Factory in you, connected. The Machinery in
me, a love algorithm. Offering a guided tour into
economisation. Into poor thinking, labelled
sensations. Calmer, less fuss, evened, glossy. I will
try not to follow the storyline, like an ant caught in a
drawn circle on a table of contents. I will name and
rename us again and again. Us?

ENVOI.

The net muddled into a Maze,
flung over the Void. Darkness. Heat.
Emptiness thickening.
Silence, fade out. Or something, still.

> 'Come on.
Darling.
Sleep, be good.
Sleep.
Sleep.
Darling.'

© LIANG YINGFEI
from *Behind the Scar*, 2019

ALL SPECIES HAVE THE SAME LIFE

Emanuele Coccia

I have forgotten everything. I have forgotten the taste and smell, and the faces of the people around me. I have forgotten the objects that filled the room on that particular day, the intensity of the light in those very first moments. Everything was too new for me to store and remember. I had to forget. I had to create a void: space for the person I was to become. To be able to perceive myself, I had to forget where I came from and the other body that had sheltered me for so long.

Birth is the absolute limit of knowledge. Beyond – before – that limit, my 'I' merges with another life. I become the same body, the same moods, the same atoms as another; another's blood circulates in my veins. The breath with which I scream when I enter the world comes from another body: a body that will never be part of me. Forgetting is not an accident. I forget so I may become myself. I forget so I may have a face.

And yet, something is preserved. Birth is not an absolute beginning. I was already something before I was born. There was me before me.

Birth is not merely the emergence of the new. It is also the absorption of the future into a past without limits. With birth, I become the involuntary vehicle of infinite previous selves: my parents, their parents, and the parents of their parents, back to the frontiers of humanity and beyond, to the frontiers of the living, and even further. I have in me the vestiges of an endless series of living beings, all born of other living beings.

I did not just forget. I was forced to forget. We live in a culture created and dominated by those who, by definition, have never had the experience of giving birth: men. This is probably why we are obsessed with death and ageing. The cult of death is the heart of our society: we reverentially archive our dead in sealed boxes, we erect mausoleums for them, we never cease to pay tribute to their memory. The grandiose reflections on death of our poets and philosophers fill entire library shelves. Birth, on the other hand, remains a mystery and a taboo. The millennial exclusion of women from the fields of speech and art means that the astonishment we feel around birth is rarely expressed. We barely talk about birth, we barely celebrate it, we barely pay attention to the traces it leaves on our bodies and selves.

So, we all forget.

And yet some of us – women – carry in our bodies the possibility of relearning what birth might mean. Women cannot recover their own birth. But they can go through birth on the other side. The antithesis of birth is not death, it is giving birth: experiencing birth 'backwards', and reversing the oblivion.

Giving birth is not just a physical event. It is not just the experience of one's body engendering another body. It is the awareness of one's body transformed into a matrix through which life passes in a pure form, stripped of the personal and individual, transmitted from self to self. Birth, from this side, is the experience of dissolving into a sea where life migrates from ego to ego. Life is revealed to be a force whose first instinct is to migrate and multiply. Any parent has acquired the knowledge of transmigration: how the self that has arrived in us from elsewhere migrates towards other destinies and other forms of life. Every self is a migrant.

That is why there can never be a single form of life. There is no unity between life and its form: birth is precisely the negation of this kind of synthesis. We always come from another form, of which we are the deformation, the variation, the anamorphosis. And every living thing can generate from its own a new form which is animated by the same life. Multiplicity is the deepest truth of life, but not in an arithmetic sense. If there is multiplicity in the living, it is because of the continuity of all beings.

In the first, microbial, stages of evolution, all species had the same life. They shared the same body and the same experiences. Everything we are now – whether we are an elephant or an oak, a lion or a mushroom – was concentrated in that same life which first detached itself from silent matter. For billions of years, this life has been transmitted from body to body, from individual to individual, from species to species, from kingdom to kingdom.

The life of any living being does not begin with its birth; it is much older. Our own life, which we imagine to be sealed within us in the most intimate and incommunicable way, does not come from us. It is not exclusive or personal. It has been transmitted to us by others, it has animated other bodies, other pieces of matter than our own. And those who passed this life down to us were not only human. Our humanity is no native or autonomous product. It is an extension and a metamorphosis of another kind of life. More precisely, it is an invention that primates drew from their own bodies, their own DNA, in order to make the life that animated them exist differently. They transmitted our form to us, and they continue to live in us. Moreover, those primates were themselves experiments launched by other species. Evolution is a grand masked ball – one that takes place in time rather than in space. Every species, from era to era, puts on a new mask, and its sons and daughters go unrecognised.

We, the living, have never stopped exchanging bodies, and what each of us is, what we call 'species', is only the set of techniques that each living being has borrowed from the others. It is because of this continuity that every species shares its fundamental traits with hundreds of others. Eyes, ears, lungs, nose, warm blood: we share these with millions of other individuals, with thousands of other species – and in all these forms, we are particularly human.

This is the deepest meaning of the Darwinian theory of evolution: species are not real. They are games of life, unstable and ephemeral configurations of a life that transits and circulates from one form to another. We have not yet drawn all the conclusions from the intuitions of Darwinism. Affirming that species are linked by heredity does not simply mean that the living constitute a family. It means, above all, that the identity of each species is purely relative: we are 'human' only in relation to apes, just as we are only offspring in relation to parents.

Every birth, in this sense, is a metamorphosis. Thanks to birth, every living body is a metamorphosis: a transformation of previous bodies. The primordial moment at which our memories run out: this is the moment of our metamorphosis. In this sense we can put to new use a story we learned as children: the caterpillar and the butterfly. Old as it is, it is still difficult to understand: one and the same life is shared by two creatures. Metamorphosis is only the mechanism that allows these two incompatible bodies to belong to the same individual. A great entomologist of the last century, Carroll M. Williams, once described the butterfly's life as schizophrenic, divided between two bodies: the first, consisting of enormous digestive tubes carried on caterpillar legs, devoted to nutrition and the future of the individual; the second, which is devoted to the future of the species, consisting of a 'flying machine devoted to sex'. According to biologists, it is precisely to prevent adults and children from competing for space and resources that the body is so radically transformed.

Every metamorphosis reveals this very strange miracle: life cannot be traced back to a precise anatomical identity. The same self can live in two incompatible bodies. This is what happens at birth. Every birth shows that life is what happens between bodies. Life is not the quality of a specific body, but what is transmitted from body to body, from world to world. Metamorphosis and birth: two bodies with nothing in common share the same life.

Metamorphosis, in fact, is the phenomenon that connects all the bodies of the world. Imagine all living bodies: not only those that belong to one species, but those that belong to all species, not only those that live now, but also those that have ever lived and those that will live in the future. They have the same relationship with each other as caterpillars and butterflies. They are the same life, transmitted from species to species.

We can go further. All living bodies share the flesh of the earth. But they also share the light of the sun.

Our earth was also 'born': it too escaped from a pre-existing body – the solar nebula – and it found its present form 4.5 billion years ago, also through the metamorphosis of matter. But the earth is entirely animated, still, by its solar parent. Look around you: the tree, that most earthly of life's expressions, retains in its carbonic flesh a light from elsewhere. Every plant is an agent of assimilation, combining the earth's mineral body with the extraterrestrial matter of the stars. An apple, a grape, a potato: they are small fragments of extraterrestrial light, encapsulated within the mineral matter of our planet. It is this light we animals seek when we eat; any act of feeding is an invisible trade of extraterrestrial light, which flows from body to body, and from species to species.

In this sense, too, we all share one life. For in every living being flows the sunlight captured by plants and stored in the mineral body of the earth. ■

COSMOS

Each night I take my boat out to you, asleep under
the oaks. I thought I saw a lotus creep out of your navel,
which means you got my cable. Remember when we were
young and the end was a black hole at the edge of forever,
a million light years away. Now we're in the thick of it.
See how it swallows everything – a jungle leopard feasting
through our bloodline of mongrels. Have you noticed,
lying there as you do in moonlight, how a hurricane viewed
from outer space looks like a wisp of cotton candy?
Or how the seagull nebula resembles a section of rosy
duodenum? Down in the market a man speaks of finding
anger in his left armpit. Another talks of space debris
drifting into the River Lethe. No one can tell me
why we paint demons on our houses, except it has
to do with entries and exits. The monsters are never
far away. I want to believe the earth is a single breathing
organism. I want to keep going with this bronze body
of mine, turning and turning the gears. You left no note,
so I must assume you woke in the middle of a dream
and took shelter in the forest. Maybe you're already
in the beauty of that other world, growing planetary rings
and gardens of foxglove. You know this skin is a thin
partition, citrus and bergamot sealed in. It's always
ourselves we're most afraid of. Take this vellum
and pin it to your bodice. Let it say we were here.

Courtesy of the author

CLARITY

Ruchir Joshi

I've spent the last five, six years, feeling I'm not getting things. At times I feel like I'm encased in some sort of prophylactic that prevents me from seeing or hearing him properly, from sensing everything I need to sense; at others it's as though he is trapped in a transparent silo and all I can do is circle around lecturing and hectoring him, all meaningless – or pointless – to use one of his favourite words.

'Why do you give a fuck? Why do you care so much?' he asks me from time to time.

'Because you're my son. Because I love you. Because I've never loved anyone more than you and your brother.' It sounds over-sweet and cheap when I play it back now in my head, but I've learned to keep what I say simple. And truthful.

Every now and then I think he's asking me this question because he himself wants to find a route to caring. At other times I think he wants to be divested of caring so much, that his love and anxiety for me, for his mother and his older brother, are too much of a burden.

Sometimes I bring up the fact that we've led these split lives since he was born. Me coming to London for a chunk of every year to be with the two of them. Them coming to India once, twice a year, first with both parents, then with their mother and then on their own, being fed into the airline system at one end by one parent, received on the landing end by the other. I tell him how I used to see them off at the airport and cry sometimes when I got home. His older brother has told me he used to miss me.

'Not me,' he says, 'I didn't think about it. Once you were gone you were gone. I thought it was normal.'

Normal. Your parents dying before you is normal, that's what they are there for, to bring you up, and then to die well before you do, leaving you to live at least some part of your life free of their presence. The same applies to you and your children, overlapping like cross-fading soundtracks: your life before parenthood, your life with your children, your children's lives after you. I'm now looking at an alternative cross-fade, my life before my younger one was born, the years with him and now life after him – which is not what I was designed for. Suddenly, I don't fit my life. Every corner is wrong, the size is suddenly incorrect, somebody else's life delivered to me by mistake, but now it's the only one available.

I was close to my own father, which many people are not. He died thirty-one years ago and I still miss him, not in a way that cripples me, but acutely nevertheless. I have vivid memories of time spent with him, of learning things, of great laughter, love and joy. I don't need to dig up those moments, they are inside me, woven into the fabric of my being. What I regret about my father's death is that it came too early. I feel sad that he never saw my sons, never played with them or watched them grow up. Then again, on days when I unsubscribe from the rational, I feel he *has* seen all this, and that he's still there, somewhere, and comes to visit from time to time. Had he lived a bit longer he would have directly exchanged sight and touch and love with his grandsons; but the way things turned out I've always felt he and the kids could only reach each other through me.

Thinking about what my son went through before he killed himself, at times I feel I didn't let enough of my father through, or of my mother either, to help him take a different route. I feel I failed as a medium – as a channel I allowed myself to be blocked.

One of the things I find myself missing is the fear. Even now I hesitate to leave my laptop where you might find it and smash it, or my mobile phone where you might take it and walk off, to listen to music, to drop it and break it, to have it slip out of your pocket and not even notice, to sell it to a dealer for a few quid's worth of some shitty low-grade shit, or my wallet with whatever small amount of cash and the house keys, which are far more important.

It's true that you never actually walked off with my phone, and the only laptops you smashed were the ones you considered your own, but one never knew: I could never take the risk, and I'm still not sure that someday you wouldn't have done to my stuff what you did to your own. But now that tension has worn thin. The putting away, the hiding of stuff, comes from habit that's now emptied of proper anxiety, and I find myself wishing it wasn't so. I find myself wishing I was still afraid.

I'm sitting on a bus when an ambulance goes by, siren on. Then a police car, roof on blue fire, going in the other direction. There's a stab of anxiety, but the knife is one of those trick ones kids play with, with a plastic blade going back into the handle. The sirens aren't for you, they can never again be for you.

Over the last five years I've rehearsed the sirens many times. Ambulance tearing through the night, me gripping your hand as you lie on the stretcher, prayers stuck in my throat, unable to break out. Police siren stopping outside the door, and then the doorbell. Me 9,000 miles away in India, too far to hear the siren, which, in fact, is what finally happens. Me not there for the police standing outside your mother's front door, no siren, just bringing the news. Me back in Calcutta when they actually come the first time, three years ago. The photos I receive of you all tubed up in the ICU – induced coma to counter huge overdose, life saved because of timely intervention – the drug traces they find coming out of you unidentifiable, Chinese whispers, outside their range of tests.

When you come out of the ICU and go back into the mental ward everybody weighs up those two bruiser-words – suicide and self-harm – and then rejects them. At the times you do admit to doing the drugs, you say you were just trying to have a blast, pushing the limits, taking this new substance, popping three small squares of this paper when you were supposed to take no more than one – because you'd read that some guy had swallowed nine and survived.

Nevertheless, over the last few years whenever I arrive from India, among the first things I always do is hide the really sharp Japanese knife and the small, lethal German paring knife in your mother's kitchen. I'm not thinking you'll use the knives on yourself, I'm not thinking that I or someone else might be at the wrong end of the blade, I'm not thinking anything specific, I'm just thinking if there was a bottle of aspirin, an electric drill or car keys I would hide those too.

RUCHIR JOSHI

When I was little I fell ill often, sometimes seriously, and each time I remember my mother praying that the illness be transferred to her. I understand that now, properly only now. It's not that I wanted to take over your 'madness', as you called it, but I often found myself wishing there was some way it could be siphoned entirely into me, like I was some kind of Neelkanth Shiva able to quarantine poison in his throat, or, like with some water-purifying plant, processed through me and out as waste.

Now the only way I can process your death, put it through the computation of my still being here and your not, is to try and think of everything as magical. Every single thing, every moment, every encounter, every sight that crosses my eyes. Everything magical, unreal, impossible and impossibly insulting to logic and reason.

You and I, we talked a lot about logic and reason. I sometimes felt that Logic-and-Reason was a faraway country that you would now and then consider visiting, but that you were not convinced by the recounting of my travels over there.

I think of the skin between the rational and the irrational. That skin that we all have, that skin of yours that got scraped away and never grew back.

The first psychiatrist who sees him is in India. I take him to the appointment when he's just turned seventeen. It's a disorder, but definitely not schizophrenia or anything long-term like that. He should get better with medication and he must stay off the illegal substances. After that it's mostly back in London where the doctors treat him. Again, no psychiatrist wants to give it a name. 'We wouldn't like to slot him into a particular condition.' But for the benefits forms they do need a label and his is 'paranoid schizophrenia'.

Some of the signs were there much earlier, but from seventeen the layers really start to thicken and surround him: whatever different brain-wiring he was carrying from birth; what the ever-present screens – TV, laptop and phone – were bringing him; the street drugs; the mental health services protocols and medication; the benefits money coming into his bank every two weeks; different nets enmeshing him, pulling him away from his mother, his brother and me, from his friends and the other grown-ups who cared desperately for him. Pulling him away from imagining a different future, one for which he might want to wake up again and again.

The anger sits close at hand, like some obsolete object now uselessly taking up space. Anger at him, at the mental health services and the ward where he accessed the more serious drugs for the first time, at the pushers and dealers circling around the wards and the streets, anger at Fuckfacebook and GlyouTube. At all these layers of netting in which he was trapped, for which I didn't have the scissors, the knives, wire cutters, laser cutters.

There was the facility for languages and accents that showed up early. A clustered gift for language, music and mathematics that was startling, almost scary. When things start to turn, the talent for language also starts biting into itself. Words become bombs, become booby traps, entanglements in which he always seems trapped. But, even in the middle of the turmoil, there are moments of crazy clarity.

In late 2013 we are in Calcutta for a couple of weeks. He is seventeen, already in pain, trying to make sense of quotidian things. He speaks nothing but his Northlondonese to everyone; he certainly speaks no Bengali. Eight months later, in London, he tells me: 'I think I'll learn Bengali.' I give some response about how he should go back to working on his Spanish, which he gave up. I tell him Bengali might be difficult to pick up. 'Hyan! *Koto* mushkil!' he sneers – 'Yes! *How* difficult!' but in a perfect Bengali accent, the sarcastic-aunty tone precise to the context. Where did he get it from?

And where did it go?

There are the scrawled notes I keep finding: 'Disbelief of Belief, Belief of Disbelief', repeatedly worked out sums between 'ego', 'traveller' and 'desire', scrawled see-saws between 'emotion' and 'thoughts', the pen pushing against commonly accepted meanings and valences of simple words, trying to map the 'I', set a net to trap the self.

Language is also a skin. My skin is different from his. When our skins rub against each other, sometimes it's like two bits of sandpaper scraping. He's angry with others about various things; with me he fights against my voice and words. His loud voice smashing into mine – same voice box; his skill with words fencing with mine – very different swords.

At some point a couple of years ago, he develops a volcanic anger at the word 'consequences', when I tell him that just as actions do, words too have consequences, like billiard balls glancing and sending each other in directions not entirely predictable.

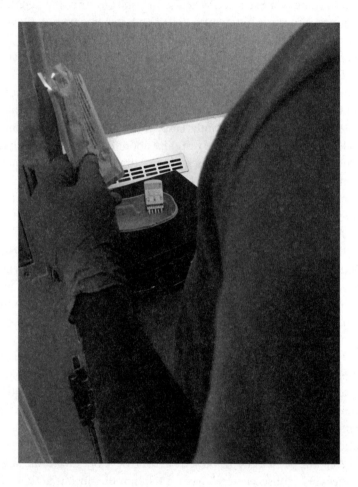

When the November 2015 attacks happen in Paris he takes it personally. 'I fucked up,' he says, 'I could have saved them.' Likewise with Trump getting elected, he takes it as his personal failure. 'I should not have let that happen.' He can handle PlayStation games all right, but the TV bothers him; often he'll ask, 'Is that live? Is that TV live?'

Through the seven-odd years of his worsening condition, there is the business of the 'signal': something getting to him that he demonstrates by rubbing together his thumb and forefinger. 'Can't you feel it? The signal?' he asks his mother, his brother, me, others. When we say we can't feel it, he explodes. 'Don't *lie*! How can you not feel it? Why are you lying to me?'

The nets tangle and tighten around him and I can't tell if it's the drugs talking or the psychosis, can't tell which comes first, the anxieties and delusions or the substances he constantly reaches for to counter them. The metaphors get tangled in my head: on the one hand there are the nets; on the other hand, layers peeling off a rain-soaked wall, first the paint of reality flaking away, then the base plaster of the will to live and finally the cement of logic, brittle now, falling out from between the bricks of words.

RUCHIR JOSHI

Sometimes I find myself thinking that by snatching yourself away, you also took away the just-walking baby I danced with, the three-year-old I read to, the eight-year-old I wrestled with, the fourteen-year-old with whom I'd argue happily about music, all those kids of mine that were you. And then I think, no, those boys were long gone, happily and correctly; and yet again no, there is nowhere those boys are going, they will always be inside me just as they would have been had you grown older and moved into your own 'normal' life.

I think of one of those Russian dolls, except this one is reversed – you open a small one and a bigger one comes out and then a bigger one from that, till your kid reaches adulthood, taller than you, walking faster than you, knowing more and knowing better than you, often looking at you with pity and fraying patience.

Maybe for a child growing up each parent is like a normal Russian doll, going down from the big, hollow, outer one to ever smaller, ever more distilled and diminishing versions. In this imbalanced yin and yang of two lives there is never a point when both parent and child are exactly the same size, or with the same power; something is always askew, always some asymmetrical osmosis taking place.

They fuck you up your girl and lad, they don't mean to but they do. They find the cracks you never had, and make some new ones too.

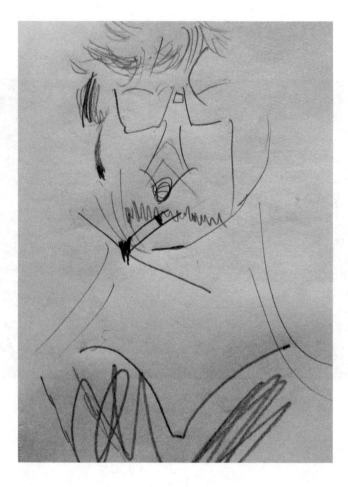

When I tell a friend about you, about your going, she – herself a mother – says, 'I don't know how you are alive after this.'

It's true. This body of mine is a strange place to be in when you're no longer in yours.

When the post-mortem reports come in three months later they find no intoxicants in your body. None of us, your mother, your brother or I, are surprised. The drugs have had their say already; we have each sensed that you did what you felt you had to do, completely stone-cold sober. For me, you had a small window of your kind of clarity and you made it pay. I wish it had been a different clarity, closer to mine.

In the garden of your mother's house in London. A warplane slicing into sky, knifing open the blue, the contrail-wound sharp for a few moments before it opens and the universe pours in. Or pours out.

In your grandmother's house near the Himalayas. I draw a portrait of you. You watch, and then you take the pencil and paper and draw one of me. ■

All photographs © Ruchir Joshi

Vladimir Mayakovsky

Already Two

It's already two a.m. You're likely asleep.
The Milky Way's a silver river through the night.
I'm in no hurry; I'll not storm your dreams
with the lightning bolts of telegrams.
'It's not you,' as they say. 'It's we.'
Love's boat has crashed on our lives.
But we've already closed out our tab,
so there's no need to list each
pain, pinprick, pang.
You watch: silence settles on the earth.
The night taxes the sky of its stars.
In such an hour one stands up and speaks
to the ages, to history, and all creation.

Translated from the Russian by Katie Farris and Ilya Kaminsky

CONTRIBUTORS

Fatin Abbas was born in Khartoum, Sudan. Her first novel, *The Interventionists*, is forthcoming from W. W. Norton.

Ida Börjel is a translator and poet. Her collections include *Skåneradio*, *The Sabotage Manuals* and *MA*.

Emanuele Coccia is Associate Professor at the École des Hautes Études en Sciences Sociales in Paris. His books include *The Life of Plants: A Metaphysics of Mixture* and *Goods: Advertising, Urban Space and the Moral Law of the Image*.

Rana Dasgupta's novels include *Tokyo Cancelled* and *Solo*, winner of the 2010 Commonwealth Writers' Prize. His non-fiction book *Capital* won the 2017 Ryszard Kapuściński Award for Literary Reportage.

Lydia Davis is the author of one novel and seven story collections, and was awarded the 2013 Man Booker International Prize.

Tishani Doshi is a poet, novelist and dancer. Her most recent books are *Girls Are Coming Out of the Woods*, shortlisted for the Ted Hughes Poetry Award, and *Small Days and Nights*, shortlisted for the Tata Best Fiction Award and a *New York Times* Bestsellers Editors' Choice.

Mark Doty's many volumes of poetry have been recognised by the National Book Award in the US and by the T.S. Eliot Prize in the UK. *What Is the Grass: Walt Whitman in My Life*, will be published in April 2020.

Katie Farris is the author of *boysgirls*, *Thirteen Intimacies* and *Mother Superior in Hell*. She is the co-translator of several books of poetry including *Gossip and Metaphysics: Russian Modernist Poems and Prose*.

Anouchka Grose is a psychoanalyst and writer practising in London. She is the author of two novels and three non-fiction books, most recently *From Anxiety to Zoolander: notes on psychoanalysis*.

Steven Heighton's most recent books are *The Nightingale Won't Let You Sleep* and *The Waking Comes Late*, which received the Governor General's Award for Poetry.

Ruchir Joshi is a writer, film-maker and the author of a novel, *The Last Jet-Engine Laugh*. His next novel, *Great Eastern Hotel*, will be published in spring 2021.

Ilya Kaminsky was born in 1977 in Odessa, former Soviet Union, and arrived in the United States in 1993 when his family was granted asylum by the American government. He is the author of *Deaf Republic* and *Dancing in Odessa*.

Kapka Kassabova is a poet and the author of *Border* and *To the Lake*, both published by Granta Books.

Anita Khemka is an artist who is a founding photographer of PHOTOINK and currently works for The MurthyNAYAK Foundation. She has been photographing Laxmi since 2003.

J. Robert Lennon is the author of two story collections, *Pieces For the Left Hand* and *See You in Paradise*, and eight novels, including *Familiar*, *Broken River* and *Mailman*, recently reissued by Granta Books.

Andrew McMillan's debut collection *physical* was the first poetry collection to ever win the *Guardian* First Book Award in 2015. His second collection *playtime* won the 2019 Polari Prize.

Vladimir Mayakovsky (1893–1930) was a Soviet activist, poet and playwright, and an important figure in the Russian Futurist movement.

Anita Roy's books include *A Year in Kingcombe: The Wildflower Meadows of Dorset* and *Gravepyres School for the Recently Deceased*.

Mahreen Sohail's fiction has appeared in the *Kenyon Review*, *A Public Space*, the *Pushcart Prize Anthology* and elsewhere. She was previously a Charles Pick South Asia Fellow at the University of East Anglia in Norwich.

Arturo Soto is a photographer and writer. His first photobook, *In the Heat*, was published in 2018.

Mónica de la Torre is the author of five poetry collections. Her most recent book, *Repetition Nineteen*, is a collection of poems and essays.

Eyal Weizman is a British Israeli architect. He is the founding director of the research agency Forensic Architecture and Professor of Spatial and Visual Cultures at Goldsmiths, University of London.

Chloe Wilson is the author of two poetry collections, *The Mermaid Problem* and *Not Fox Nor Axe*. She won the 2019 *Iowa Review Award* in Fiction and was shortlisted for the 2017 Commonwealth Short Story Prize.

Esther Woolfson is the author of *Corvus: A Life with Birds* and *Field Notes From a Hidden City*, both published by Granta Books. 'Between Light and Storm' is taken from her book of the same name, to be published by Granta Books in 2020.